When I Was Just Your Age

When I Was Just Your Age

Robert Flynn and Susan Russell

UNIVERSITY OF NORTH TEXAS PRESS~DENTON

Requests for permission to reproduce material from this work should be sent to:
Permissions
University of North Texas Press
P. O. Box 13856
Denton, Texas 76203-3856

The paper in this book meets the minimum requirements of the American National
Standard for Permanence of Paper for Printed Library materials, z39.48-1984.

Library of Congress Cataloging-in-Publication Data

Flynn, Robert, 1932–
When I was just your age / by Robert Flynn and Susan Russell
p.   cm.
Includes index.
Summary: As they reminisce about their childhood, thirteen interviewees chronicle life
in Texas and other parts of the West during the early part of the twentieth century.
ISBN 0-929398-39-4
1. United States–Social life and customs–20th century–juvenile literature. 2. Interviews–
United States–Juvenile literature. 3. Oral history–Juvenile literature. [1. United States–
Social life and customs–20th century. 2. Texas–Social life and customs. 3. Interviews.] I.
Russell, Susan, 1946–   . II. Title.
E 169.R956   1992
973.91'092–dc20
[B]   92-15460
CIP
AC

To those who told their stories
and to the children who asked and listened.

Contents

FOREWORD

A democracy—which depends for survival on an informed electorate, sufficiently interested in the nation to exercise the franchise—owes intrinsic obligations to its youth. In the turbulent climate of today's society, where long held assumptions are beginning to fray, children lack the security of ritual institutions and the guidance of memory. They yearn for the values that will not fail them. It behooves us to provide all our children with the aspects of their environment which auger stability, solace and inspiration. We must give them a sense of place, a feeling of belonging to the past and the future, as well as the present, and a recognition of beauty and order. We must confer on them a responsibility for their place of being, which inevitably fosters a love of country.

—Margaret Cousins

ACKNOWLEDGMENTS

Grateful acknowledgment is made to:

The Learning About Learning Foundation and the original staff who created the "Thinking Historically" curriculum: Jearnine Wagner, Julia Jarrell, Susie Monday and Cindy Herbert.

The National Endowment for the Humanities, for making it possible.

The Alice Kleberg Meyer Foundation, whose generous assistance allowed us to expand the program into a book.

The children who traveled with us to collect additional interviews: Rana Emerson, Benjamin Espy, Thomas Espy and Cory Russell.

INTRODUCTION

History is gathered from documents, artifacts and memory. Of these three, memory is the one that serves when the subject is childhood, and that is why we have made "memories" the focus of this book.

When I Was Just Your Age began as part of the Humanities program of The Learning About Learning (LAL) Educational Foundation in San Antonio, Texas. LAL developed ways of actively and personally connecting children to the past. Those experiences helped children perceive patterns of behavior, how people invented their lives and in a larger sense their culture.

In 1985, the National Endowment for the Humanities funded a project called "Thinking Historically," that is, the process of seeing oneself as a part and product of all that has happened before. To enter that past, the children collected oral histories. They learned how oral stories differ from written ones, how Native American stories, for instance, have a less linear development than the stories they were accustomed to reading or hearing in school. They began to recognize the "quick" of the story. They encountered real diversity. They discovered that families can be "rich" in some things while being "poor" in others. They gained new perspectives.

The results of this project were so valuable that we decided to expand the effort into a book. Curious about geographical differences, we traveled around the state along with several children who were, by now, veteran interviewers. Together, we collected the stories of a variety of Texans, all focusing on childhood. These remembrances gave us not only a picture of everyday life, with its chores, habits and holidays, but also a reflection of the beliefs of the time, the responses to the land, the sense of community and the impact these things made over a lifetime. Family photographs were collected to complement the oral histories. They were important to understanding the atmosphere of the time and place. We included many of them here as we gathered the interviews into a book.

The activity guide at the end of the book is designed to give children, parents and teachers ideas for discovering and collecting the remarkable historical material that surrounds them. We hope it will enrich the present and the future.

Robert Flynn and Susan Russell

Eloise Benavides

Born in Mexico, Eloise Benavides moved to Texas as a young child. Although she knew little English, she refused to be placed in the slower class when she went to school. That determination to succeed and interest in education has remained with her. Her adult career has been spent as a teacher and school administrator in San Antonio.

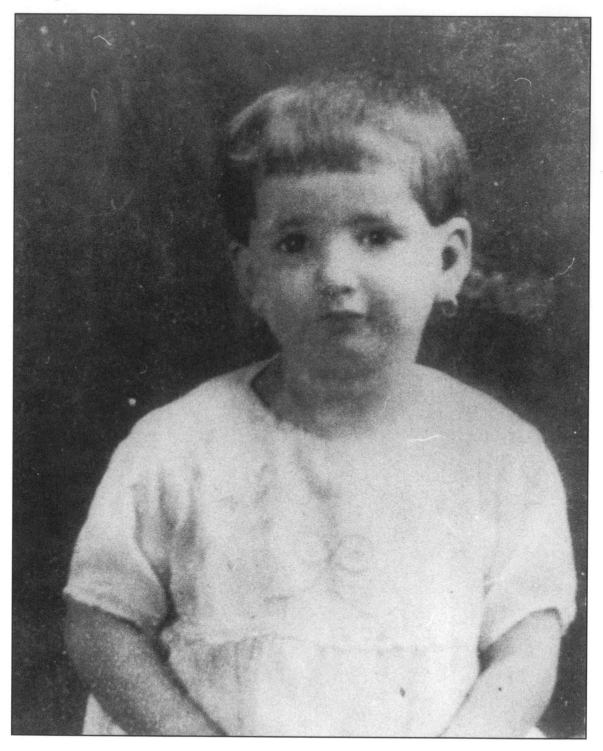

Eloise Benavides

Where were you born?

I was born in Monterrey, Mexico. I was brought to the United States when I was three years old. We came by train, my mother, three brothers, three sisters and I. My father stayed behind for business reasons and my mother brought the children with her. I remember that my mother got very scared. I couldn't understand what was wrong, but later she told us that some man tried to snatch her purse. The conductor stopped the train and she got her purse back. I also remember my grandmother crying when we left. That's about as far back as I can remember.

In the beginning we came to Saspamco, a very little town between Elmendorf and Floresville. If you wink you miss it. We were used to a city, Monterrey. In Saspamco there was only

3

one paved street. It was like a wilderness and we were sort of isolated there. We didn't stay there long but I did start to school there. I didn't know any English whatsoever and it was very difficult for me to understand the teachers.

Were there bilingual classes?

There were no bilingual classes then. That's why I am so in favor of bilingual education. I understand why. I was not a dumb kid. They divided the classes into the A, B, and C and they wanted to put me in the lower class. I was too proud and I didn't want to be in the lower class. Every time they assigned me there, I wouldn't move. I knew the teacher was telling me to move because she was using sign language, but I acted like I didn't understand because I didn't want to be in the dumb class. I wanted to be in the smart class. They had to bring my older brother from a higher class to come and move me and he had to lift me with the chair because I wouldn't move. As soon as my brother left, I moved back to where I was before, so the teacher gave up.

I tried. I studied. My dad and mother were proud people. I didn't want to make a B. When we moved to San Antonio, I received a gold pin for students maintaining grades no lower than a B throughout high school. My mother was in the hospital and my dad was managing the store, and I had no one to take

Eloise's father and mother.

me. We were supposed to wear an evening dress and my mother had made a lovely long dress. I borrowed a bicycle from a neighbor and rolled my dress as much as I could and used clothes pins to hold it up and rode to Brackenridge High School. I parked the bicycle in front, put a rope around it because I didn't have a chain, put my dress down, walked across the stage, got my pin, raised my dress again with clothespins and rode home.

Did the songs your mother sang influence your life?

They did. I learned a lot about the arts. I did not inherit her voice, but I love music and I love to paint and draw. Her songs taught me that when you are sad and you hear good music you feel good inside. When you feel tired, turn to your music. Many of her songs taught a moral lesson.

Did your family sing and read together?

Yes. Music was important when we were growing up. It kept the family

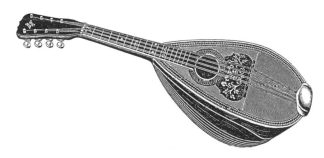

together. We used to do a lot of singing after dinner. In a lot of games that we played singing was essential. My oldest brother, Joe, played the harmonica. My brothers, Alphonso and Nick, accompanied him by banging on a tub, like a drum. It was a lot of fun. My sisters, Consuelo, Isabel, Ester and I, tried to sing along.

My mother played the mandolin and sang nursery rhymes to us when we

were growing up and later she sang classical songs. "La Golondrina" she used to put us to sleep. "The Song of the Swallows" was a beautiful song. There was a little poem she would sing about the ants, how hard they labor and how organized they are. I think she did this to help her eight children become organized. She used to say, "Muevete. Move. If you don't do anything, just move. When you move you are doing something." Keeping us busy was very wise because we hardly had time for getting into mischief or thinking evil thoughts.

Eloise's father and mother.

After dinner my mother used to read to us. She brought books from Mexico and she kept the family together by singing, playing games, and reading stories to us. I remember the story "Corazon de un niño," "The Heart of a Child," by Amado Nervo, about the hardship of a child growing up in a very poor family. She would read us a chapter and act out the parts and expressions and we all cried. But we enjoyed it. Since both of my parents were well educated in Mexico, they knew the value of a well-rounded education and they knew that education begins in the home.

Eloise sitting on her father's lap

What occupation was your father in?

My father had a grocery store at 203 Labor Street. We lived on Mt. Zion. They tore the house down for the Victoria Courts Housing Project. That's when we moved to the back of dad's grocery store. My dad had the store for fifty years.

Did you help in the grocery store?

I started helping my father in the grocery store when I was knee-high to a grasshopper. I used to sell candy, and I ate a lot of it. The candy disappeared and my father wondered why.

He never had an adding machine in his store. He did it always in his head and he was quicker than an adding machine and never made an error. His speed and accuracy were amazing. At first some customers would question his accuracy and go back and total it again, and every time they would say, "El Señor Nicolas es perfecto en matematicas." I think they should be strict in teaching mathematics.

Did you get paid?

No. Nowadays, children get an allowance. I don't ever remember asking for or being offered an allowance. It was expected of us to help and we benefited from whatever goods we received. My father did not know any English, which made it difficult for him to run his store at first, but he did not let the language barrier get him down. He had a wife and eight children to support. He would write on a clipboard on the wall "pan" and next to it "bread," "leche" next to "milk", etc. It was difficult for him to learn English, but he did, and became an American citizen.

Were you an American citizen?

We were all Mexican citizens, except my youngest brother, Ramiro, who was born in Saspamco. When my brothers volunteered for service in World War II

they automatically became American citizens. I said I was going to apply for work at Kelly Field in Civil Service and also become a citizen. They told me there were regulations and I could not work in Civil Service until I became an American citizen. I became an American citizen, but I never worked at Kelly Field.

Were you affected by the depression?

There were eight children in the family, and during the depression it was hard to get by. I remember we didn't have a lot of things that my children and my grandchildren have. But we were happy because we were so close, and did so many things together. My mother would wake us up at five in the morning on Saturday to take a walk and pick wildflowers. I used to keep a little box with all kinds of bugs.

We walked in the woods and went swimming. Also the railroad tracks were right in back of our backyard. In our family the older one would take care of the younger one.

Sometimes the train was there for days. We climbed on the train and played for hours and nobody disturbed us. Sometimes they would have a boxcar of sand and we had the biggest sandbox in the world. One day we were making sand castles and the train started moving. I dropped my little sister off the train and jumped. Our guardian angels worked full

Medicinal Herbs

Anis or Anise is an herb grown mainly for its seeds, which have a warm, spicy taste. The seed is the only part of the plant used and it is used mostly for making tea. Anise combined with oregano and boiled with sugar or honey is used for coughs.

Manzanilla or chamomile, a perennial, is part of the thistle family. The flowers look much like daisies. The flowers and leaves have a sweet smell but bitter taste. Manzanilla tea is used for head colds and colic. When cool the tea is used for inflammation of the eyes. Use one teaspoon of dried flowers per cup of water, bring to boil and simmer.

Zabila or Aloe Vera has been traced back thirty-five hundred years. The gelatin-like substance in the center of the leaves is used for healing open wounds, meat tenderizer, wrinkle remover, arthritis, rheumatism, stomach disorders, insect bites, scratches, burns, cuts and acne.

time. My mother never knew about it. She would have skinned me alive. My parents did not believe in spanking. But they were strong believers in lecturing.

We used to do laundry in the river. One time my mother almost drowned. My oldest sister saw my mother drowning. She yelled for my father. Mother had beautiful long hair and that's how my father pulled her out and saved her life. I was afraid of going in the river but I overcame the fear and became a good swimmer.

What were some of the major illnesses?

When we lived in Saspamco, my brother, number five in the family, had diphtheria and my mother was worried that the rest would get it because we hadn't been inoculated. There were no hospitals in that town and we had to go to Floresville to the hospital. They saved his life, and we were all inoculated.

I don't remember getting seriously ill. I did get the mumps but that was after we moved to San Antonio and I was going to St. Michael's. I couldn't swallow anything and when Sister Visitation saw me, I could hardly talk. Sister Visitation said, "Are you sick?" And I said, "No." I didn't want to miss school. She said, "You look very pale." I said, "I look fine, Sister." She said she was going to call my parents and she did. She was afraid I was going to give mumps to the others.

I didn't want to stay home the amount of days they made you stay when you had the mumps, so I tried to come back early. When Sister Visitation saw me, she said, "You look terrible. Go back home for another week." They used to give us lemon to swallow and if you couldn't swallow then they knew you had the mumps because it really hurts. They cut the lemon in half and let you take a little bit and if you couldn't swallow, you had to go back home.

My mother knew so many home remedies. She boiled manzanilla tea for stomach ache, relaxing, for any ailment. That's what Peter Rabbit got when he overate at Mr. McGregor's garden. And mint. She used to boil mint, and anise, and many other herbs and spices which smelled and tasted delicious.

She boiled pecan leaves and gave us the brew from the leaves to strengthen the blood. For stomach ache she gave us chamomile tea. There was yerba anise tea. There was a real bitter tea, estafiate, that she used when nothing else worked. For a fever there was a plant they called boraja. It had a lavender purple flower. She made it into a tea and we would drink it.

If you had the hiccups they would give you a piece of red thread to put on your forehead and the hiccups would go away. For earaches she used a little green leaf that had a yellow bloom that she put on the back of the ear. If we

Eloise as a young woman.

had what they called air in our ears, they would make a funnel out of paper, and they would stick the end of the funnel in our ear and then they would put the other end on fire. It drew the air out.

If we got spooked, "espanto," they said we were under a spell. Mother would build a fire outside, and put a pot on the fire. She'd throw these herbs in there and the water would start boiling. Then she would throw her wedding ring in there, and it would go fissss, like that, and that shocked you back.

They believed babies should wear the socket of a deer eye around their neck. Mothers would put a little lace border around the eye. They would draw a hole through it and pass a little ribbon

9

through it, and as long as the baby was wearing that it was protected from the evil eye.

If you were not protected, and not lucky, they would take a raw egg and rub it all over your body. Then they would crack the egg and put it in a saucer and if the child had the evil eye, the center would show the evil eye. That was the diagnosis. The treatment depended on who was giving it to you. Mother would take lime and while she was praying, she would put that lime on the ground in the form of a cross. Then she made a broom out of twigs, and there must have been herbs in there, and she would sweep me all over my body with that broom while she was praying. We were healthy. I don't remember going to the doctor very often.

Eloise and her sisters

What was the church like when you were little?

My parents were very religious and made it a point that we had religion at home. We had to attend mass and everyone made communion. My brothers served as altar boys. My parents invited the priests for Sunday dinner at our house. I loved going to church because we would meet friends there. I remember when the nun asked me who was Pope. It was Pope Pius XI. I didn't speak much English, but I wanted to answer because I always tried to excel. I overheard someone say Pope Pius, and I said it too, except I said "Popeye." I couldn't understand why they laughed.

My father didn't get to go to mass with us every time because he was running the store. I used to ask him about it. "You make us go to church. How come you aren't sinning by not going?" He said, "The altar is right here for me, because I have eight children to feed and God understands." Since the other stores were closed, it was his best day for business.

What about hobbies and sports?

I was one of the best roller skaters. I used to roller skate from Labor Street to Edgar Allen Poe School through all kinds of sidewalks, cracked, broken, rough, dry, wet. We never rode the bus. We walked or skated. One day we had a hail storm and it was like snow, about a foot and a half high. We stopped at a Chinaman's store at the corner of Hackberry and Victoria Street and asked him for cardboard boxes and put them on our heads and ran home.

We couldn't afford rackets, but I loved to play tennis. Every chance that I got in school I played tennis. At the Poe school we had tournaments and I used to play when I was in school. At school they had rackets, but ours were wood. My older brother made them.

What other games did you play?

We used to play tag, and hide and seek, and jacks. My mother taught us many singing games like "A la Rueda de San Miguel," something like "Ring Around the Rosy." There was a popular song, "In the Isle of Capri That I've Met You." Ester and I would climb way up on a limb and we would just sing and have fun until Mother called us to dinner.

We used to roll barrels standing on top of them. A few feet from our house there were thousands of "barrels," that were really clay pipes for sewers or whatever. They stacked them in rows and my sister and I used to run on top of them and jump from one row to another. Afterwards we realized we could have fallen and been hurt but we never thought of that.

We did a lot of walking in the woods, but we never did encounter a snake. I guess we never bothered them and they never bothered us. We didn't go around killing animals or anything like that. Everything was natural. Mother knew the older ones would take care of the younger ones.

My happiest days were then, in my childhood, because at a certain hour we had to go to bed. Mother used to read to us and tell stories. She told us how my father courted her. They didn't have dating. They saw each other at church on Sunday, or maybe a family picnic and that's how they got to talk. My father used to write poems on cards and send them to my mother. She showed me three or four beautiful cards but I couldn't make out what language it was. She explained that my father wrote everything backwards so that her mother and father wouldn't know what was going on. She would hold them to a mirror to read them.

She told us how La Llorona, the wailing woman, had a nervous breakdown. She killed her four little ones and she cut them up and threw them in the river. Afterwards when she came to her senses she wanted them back, and there was no way she could bring them back. After midnight, the wailing woman comes out, and if you go to a river you can hear her. I could hear her. It was a horrible scream. Mother would tell us this story and no matter how many times she told it to us, tears would run down my cheeks, but I loved every minute of it.

She told us the one about La Mano Pachona, which was about a big fat hand, and you better behave, otherwise that hand would get you. There were so many stories, games, adventures. That's why I remember the beautiful things about my parents, my family, childhood. We were very poor, the water was outside, but there were so many stories, so many good and unforgettable times.

Horton Foote

Horton Foote, who wanted to be an actor, has become perhaps Texas's most distinguished writer. Two of Foote's screenplays, *To Kill A Mockingbird*, and *Tender Mercies,* have received Academy Awards for screenplays. Born in Wharton, Texas, Foote has written about his hometown with love, understanding and honesty.

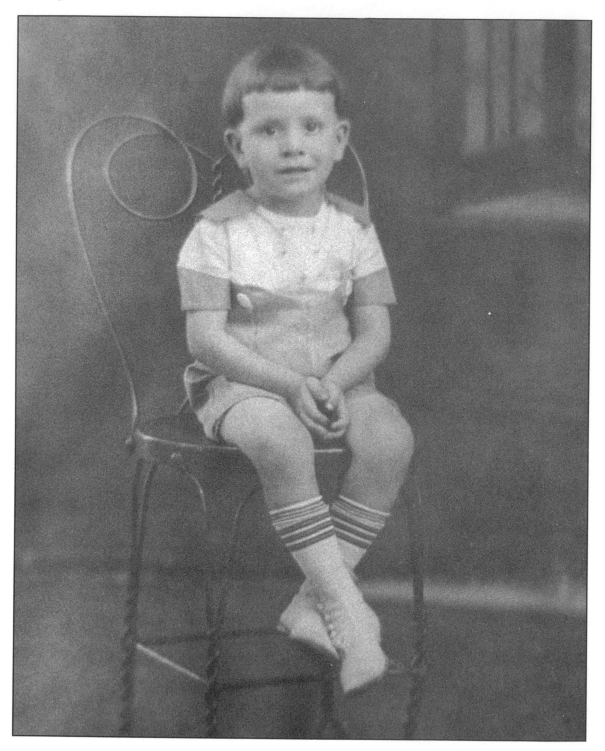

Horton Foote

Tell me about the pecan tree in your front yard.

The tree was planted the year I was born, 1916. It's not a native. There was some grafting because the pecans at the beginning were very large and now they've diminished in size. It's gone through at least fifteen hurricanes that I know of. You know, pecan trees are not the deepest rooted trees in the world. The one over there, which you can see through the window, is a native, but I think it's at least 150–200 years old. There are a lot of native pecans here. All the trees in our backyard are trees that rooted themselves and have grown

15

considerably in my lifetime. When I was a boy we had no trees in the backyard except some fig trees and a chinaberry tree, because my father loved chickens. We had chickens in the back. They kept anything from growing on it.

This is part of a large tract of land that belonged to my grandfather. There were cotton fields all around it from here to town. On this side was his lot where he kept his horses and cows and whatever. The house was a kind of peace offering. My mother and father had eloped to get married. Before I was born, they all made up, and my grandfather built this house for my momma. It's in her name. My father was a very proud man. He didn't have a lot of money. He didn't want people to think he was marrying her for her money, so he wouldn't let his name be on the deed. Its entirely in her name. Of course I don't remember it, but I was told we moved here when I was not quite one year old. And this was the center of my life, all my growing up. It was the very world.

This house then has also survived a number of hurricanes.

Oh yes. This house is wonderfully built. As a matter of fact, it's built out of cypress, which is the hardest wood that you can have. The floors are pine but the main house is cypress. But we never stayed here during a hurricane. We had a storm house out back. It's still out there,

Horton's home.

but we never used it. We always went to my grandmother's—our backyards are back to back. It's an enormous house and I always felt more than just security. The storms were a time of great excitement because many of our relatives from the deep coast would come in to get away from the hurricanes. This is called the Gulf Coast, but we're really forty miles from the coast. It was a very sociable time. I got to stay up late and everybody talked half the night with nobody getting much sleep.

Horton's grandparent's house.

It was like Christmas, despite all the destruction going on around us. They'd speculate, and tell about other storms, always about the 1900 storm. It was always the focus of everybody's stories— when the waves got to the top of the Galvez Hotel or something spectacular like that. When the sea wall broke down.

Everybody slept on pallets. All that kind of stuff that appeals to a child. The electricity was off. The water was off. We drew water and had it in reserve in case. The storms didn't usually last more than a day and a half, I think. The dramatic time was at night. I heard all those sounds.

I always remember when it stopped and we dared go outside. The landscape had changed, the sky was broken, and it seemed so peaceful. And then, all this destruction around. Tree limbs, chicken coops, parts of houses. I don't think anything was better than my grandmother's house. It was superbly built. It had an enormous gallery which is four times as wide as here, almost all around the house. My father took me out on that gallery once during a storm. Held me tight, you know.

We also have enormous floods around here. That was almost as much fun as a hurricane to a child, because the water sometimes would come up to the top steps out there. We'd have to take a boat to go to town. The floods lasted until I think the late 20's, early 30's.

There was a raft in the river that evidently caused these floods. My grandfather was in charge of that for years, head of the Raft Commission. I suppose he must have gotten rid of it some way.

Horton's grandfather.

Your father had a store and was also a farmer?

My father had a bit of a struggle because our whole economy depended on cotton, which I learned early. It was the first thing I learned to ask. "How's the cotton?" My earliest memory of my father was walking out with him and looking at the skies to see if it was going to rain or not.

My father didn't actually farm. None of us have farmed. He managed my grandparent's cotton farm. We had tenants. My father walked to town to the store every day. None of these houses were here. There was a dirt road among all the cotton fields, and he'd walk down the dirt road; we had lots of cats and the cats would always come to meet him when he came home at night because he'd bring them food. It was a very quiet life. Father was a great walker. On Sundays, he'd get on the railroad track and walk the track out to Glen Flora, which is a small town about eight miles away. Often at night he took walks.

He had a garden out back, and his chickens. The reason I think he was so fond of chickens was that his family was victim of the Reconstruction and all that. They didn't have much money after that, although his great-grandfather, Albert Clinton Horton, was the first lieutenant governor of Texas. He was from Alabama. He came here and had a great plantation, and at the time of the Civil War, he had 120 slaves. He was a man of great wealth. He also owned a house outside of Austin with a lot of land around it, and a house at Matagorda. My father grew up with people pointing and saying, "This used to belong to us, that used to belong to us." Which is a terrible thing to grow up with. His father and mother separated and his mother took him to live with her. She took in boarders. She had no money. My father had some pet chickens, and without telling him, she cooked the chickens for Christmas dinner. He got violently ill and no one knew what it was. I'm sure he was just heartbroken about those pets of his. He had chickens a great deal of his life.

Did you have any chores as a child?

No, unfortunately. In those days you could get servants for $1.50 to $2.00 a week. I think in some ways it was a great deprivation to the wealthy. It made them not very self-reliant. I didn't do much as a child, except to play, before the age of ten. I'd come home for dinner, and then I would take my father his dinner on the trip back to school.

From the age of ten on, I worked with my father at the store. It was a valuable experience, particularly on non-Saturday days. Saturday was the busy day; now it's just like any other day downtown. On weekdays I'd come in after school, or in the summertime, and the old timers would come in and visit. His store was headquarters for them. Everybody was either semiretired or retired, loafing around town and constantly retelling how it was and who did this and no, you're wrong, and who did that.

Albert Clinton Horton

Albert Clinton Horton, born in Georgia, 1798, moved to Alabama and served in the Alabama Senate, 1832. In 1834, he moved to a plantation in Wharton County, Texas. He returned to Alabama in 1835 and with James Butler Bonham organized the Mobile Grays, all of whom died in the Goliad Massacre in 1836. Horton, who had been sent to scout a crossing on Coleto Creek, escaped the massacre. He served in the Senate of the Republic of Texas and was the first lieutenant governor of the State of Texas. He served as acting governor of Texas while Governor James Pinckney Henderson commanded troops during the Mexican War. He was considered one of the wealthiest men in the state but the Civil War wrecked his fortune. He was buried at Matagorda in 1865.

What are some of your other childhood memories?

I heard about the flu epidemic of 1918 all my life. It was a very real thing for me. I was born then, but I was just a baby. But my father and mother both had the flu. He had a very bad case. Neither of them could do for each other. He had a recurrence of it, and nobody could come over, until finally this great-

19

aunt who was a nurse came and stayed with us. So many people died. And those names were always recounted.

During the first World War there were certain German families in town that wouldn't put up the American flag. Everyone was scandalized.

But the first World War wasn't as interesting to me as the Civil War. That was my war. That was the war that engaged my attention. That was the war I wanted to be in.

People around me were still talking about that war, and certainly the great storytellers were. A lady across the street would go on for hours about it. She had a favorite story about the Yankees coming in and saying, "Blood or gold, blood or gold."

They took all her silver and things. Those stories charmed me.

We played Southerners and Yankees. Nobody wanted to be the Yankees, so we made the little kids be Yankees. There was a lady across the street from my grandmother's house who was a great Confederate buff. Her grandfather was Col. J.P. Rogers—I think at the Battle of Corinth. She had a Confederate uniform, and she'd tell us these wild stories about the war. The name Lincoln was not mentioned. Once I came home and announced that the teacher had asked who was right, the North or the South, and I think she unfortunately said the North.

There was a house built across the way that had two boys and we played together a great deal. They were the sons of architects so they were good with their hands, and they could do things with Erector sets and stuff like that, that frustrated me. We used to climb that great pecan tree and build tree houses up there. We would string

Horton's father.

wires from one tree to the other and hold on to an iron pipe and slide from one tree to the other. I loved to climb. That's the thing I remember most. Sliding down those wires, and climbing up on garages and in trees. I loved to be up in trees.

20

I don't know why my parents allowed that, careful as they were about many things. They'd never let me go into town because my father was raised on the streets, and he had a horror of them. But they gave me great freedom here. We also used to build caves. The boy across the street from my grandmother's house had an enormous backyard. That's

Horton's mother.

where we dug our caves. There was an old creek, which often was not running. We would get way down deep, digging out holes. I was a great admirer of Tom Sawyer and Huck Finn and I thought I was Tom Sawyer in my cave.

My friends' father managed the oil mill and cotton gin and we would play on top of the cotton bales, jumping around and running on those bales. We weren't athletically inclined. As I got older I played some baseball, but growing up we did more imaginative things. We didn't organize things. Mostly climbing, and bicycles, and a lot of skating when we got sidewalks.

I loved unique pets and was dying to have beehives. I found out where I could get a queen bee and I just nagged my father to death. He wouldn't let me. Very early on I got guinea pigs, which you couldn't get in Wharton. You had to take the train to El Campo. Then I had a horse which I rode. They never teach you how to ride horses down here. They just put me on the back of the horse and said, "Go." I'd run the horse and then I'd come home and water it. Nobody told me that was bad for a horse. Well, this poor thing, I winded him so, that when I went off to school, they sent him out to one of the farms, and they killed him because he was ruined. I never have forgotten that.

What did you do at night?

We always had supper together. My father didn't come home for dinner, but we always waited for him to have supper. In the summer, spring, and fall we played outside until dark. We played school on the steps at night, and one by

21

one, we'd kind of drop off. Mother and Father and all my relatives were great talkers. They'd usually sit out on the front gallery and talk. I listened to them, and then when I'd get in bed I could hear them talking away. I spent a lot of my life listening. All kinds of stories. Constantly told, retold. So the days when I wasn't on this earth were as real to me as the days that I was. And as vivid. This cycle of plays that I'm working on include a lot of things that I heard right there.

When I did that scene in "To Kill A Mockingbird" which is not in the book—the essence is in the novel but the physical location is not—when the sheriff comes to tell that there's some trouble in the town, I have the two children in the room listening, and the father and the sheriff don't know they're listening. I took that example from here because that's what I used to do. I listened to things children weren't supposed to hear.

You were more a collector of stories than a teller of stories?

Much, much more. I was in a very aggressive household. Everybody was always interrupting one another and retelling the story, and I soon learned that a story could have about five different versions. A theme and variations, like a jazz riff. When I got up north, I used to entertain my friends with stories on my relatives and people that I had known. I

began to carry the stories on. I've always had an abiding interest in this place. Some deep kinship. From the time I started writing it never occurred to me to write about anything else. In mysterious ways I think my material has chosen me.

When did you decide to be a writer?

That was one of those decisions I kind of eased into. I had this terrible urge to act. I didn't want to go to college, I wanted to go to dramatic school. I had just turned sixteen when I graduated. I suspect in Wharton they thought it strange that a boy would want to go off and be an actor. It worried my father considerably. I don't know now why he let me go.

They saw I wasn't going to give up, so they put me on the bus from Houston to Los Angeles. I had an aunt in Dallas and stopped over, and got back on the bus, and saw my first mountains, and got to Los Angeles. I stayed at the Y in Pasadena until I could go to the school, which didn't open until the following Monday, so I had to learn fast about life. At the school I could hardly be understood, I had such an accent, and the first thing they threw me into was Roman Comedy. I don't know how I survived.

I don't think I really wanted to be an actor, I wanted to be a movie star. But my grandmother came out and took me to see three Ibsen plays and that changed my life. I saw that and I thought, this is what I want to do. I gave up wanting to be a movie star after that, and concentrated on acting in plays.

I went to New York and retrained. There was a group of people there, older, more sophisticated, and they decided to start an off-off Broadway theater and invited me to join. We called ourselves the American Actors Company because we were doing American plays.

Agnes De Mille came and was going to do a compilation of dances and sketches and one-act plays and call it "The American Legend." We were doing improvisations with each other, helping each other understand different regions, and I did an improvisation called "The Hurricane." Agnes said, "You seem to be in touch with a certain kind of Texas life; you should try writing a play." I came back to this house and wrote a play called "Texas Town," in which I had the lead.

The Humphrey-Weidman Company had a theater which we rented and opening night the New York critics and Lee Strasberg and Clifford Odets and people like that came. They liked the play except they didn't like my acting very much. That kind of threw me. That summer the American Actors Company went away as a company but I got some wonderful parts. Whatever need I had to act got fulfilled that summer and I began to switch.

After two other plays off-Broadway which were well received, I had a play on Broadway but it didn't work. It ran about two months but I wasn't getting any royalties, so I had to go to work in a bookstore. There I met my wife, which was a nice dividend; I wouldn't have met her otherwise.

We decided to get out of New York and we started a theater in Washington. It lasted about four years and that was the chance I had to experiment and work and get to know something about my craft and not have the New York critics breathing down my neck. In that period I finished "The Chase," and I got a job teaching at the American Theater Wing, and writing for the Goodyear Playhouse and Playhouse 90. That's really how I got started.

What values do you think have been passed down through generations in your family?

My father didn't like guns. We were never allowed to have guns. The line from "The Trip to Bountiful" I took from life: "My father was a peculiar man. He would never allow guns because he loved birds." My father wouldn't let anyone bring a gun on this place.

My father taught me great respect for honesty and honest work. Once, I think he was worried because he had to work so hard everyday that we never had time together. He asked me what I wanted to do, and I told him I wanted to go to the picture show. We took the train to Houston and we went to the Kirby in the morning, and the Majestic in the afternoon, and the Metropolitan at night, and got back on the train and came home. I know he didn't care much about it. He did it out of sheer love for me.

There was a deep love in our family, a great sense of kinship which always made me feel very secure. I was loved. Some of my relatives felt that it was a very binding thing. I never felt that.

We didn't have a lot of money. I didn't know this until later, but my father had to sell a rent house to pay my tuition to dramatic school. I've seen many a day that there's been no more than seventy-five cents in the cash register. Then maybe on a Saturday, he had only $60. I've seen my father's worried face. I know he had to go to the bank and borrow money, and he always dreaded going. There were days when he didn't think he could keep the store open. They never hid things. I could see what the store had taken in. I could hear them talking, and I could hear them get discouraged.

My mother tried to cheer Father up. They were very close. I knew that anything we didn't have was not because of a lack of love. And really, what does a young boy need?

Maury Maverick, Jr.

Maury Maverick, Jr., is a member of an illustrious family with ties to both the American Revolution and the War for Texas Independence. A lawyer and former state legislator and college professor, Maverick has been more interested in justice than the law. He has become a successful columnist and has discovered that of his careers, he likes writing best.

Maury Maverick, Jr.

Where did the word "maverick" originate?

It came from my great-grandfather, Samuel Augustus Maverick. He came to San Antonio in 1835. He was not a cattle-man, but somebody paid off a debt to him with cattle which he put on an island out in the Gulf of Mexico. When the tide went out, the cattle could go ashore. He didn't bother to brand them, so they would say, "There go old Maverick's cows."

The way the word got around the world is that cattlemen would come to Corpus Christi to pick up cattle, and the cows that weren't branded they called them mavericks. So they took the cattle to South America and called them "maverico." In India, Kipling, the great poet, used the word one time: "The charge of the mavericks."

So that's how the word got around, and it means unbranded. In the contemporary political sense it would mean some person who doesn't run with the herd. He might be liberal or even radical, politically.

Where did your ancestors come from?

The Mavericks came from England, Barbados Island, and one branch went to Boston and one branch went to South Carolina.

Last year I was lecturing at Harvard and I went to the old burial ground. The first battle for independence of this country was the Boston Massacre. The young people, not much older than you are, were throwing rocks at the British soldiers. They called the British soldiers "Lobster Backs" because the uniforms had a red back and looked like a lobster. One of the people killed, a seventeen-year-old boy named Samuel Augustus Maverick, was a distant cousin. I went to visit his grave and started crying.

My first name is Maury, a French name, and on that side my people came from Virginia. They were Huguenots, which is a French term for Protestant. They were Episcopal preachers. One of them was Thomas Jefferson's preacher, and Mr. Jefferson indicated that Reverend James Maury was so narrow-minded and old-fashioned that he drove him into forming the Unitarian Church of America.

What was it like for you growing up in San Antonio?

I went to schools here in the city. Lamar Elementary School by Menche Park. I was one of the few Anglo kids at Hawthorne. We were in the minority in those days. Then I went to Texas Military Institute. My father was in Congress, and I didn't want to live in Washington so I boarded at the military school. I went to high school and played football but wasn't any good at it. I was on the third string. I was a commencement debater, made grades of about C+. I wasn't a very good student.

I barely remember the depression. My father, during that time, was the Tax Collector-Assessor of Bexar County. He was making eight thousand dollars a year, which is not a lot of money now, but it was then. My father and mother set up a place where people would get off the train and provided them with freight cars to sleep in. It was a commune for poor people and I remember it was pretty bad. Those were hard days, but in many ways they were also pleasant days because San Antonio was smaller.

Once, my father brought back two javelinas from Mexico and named them

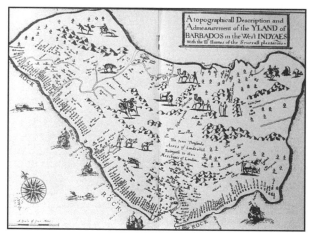

Barbados, West Indies.

Maury's parents.

Miss Hupperitz, there. I'm still scared of her. She caught me throwing an apple core at a car passing by and so she took me inside and made me put my fingers out and hit each knuckle with a ruler. When she was dying in a Catholic hospital on the south side, St. Benedict's, I left some flowers for her. She was a wonderful lady. Republican, very conservative, and she gave me the dickens. She deeply touched my life. She taught me about discipline and good manners.

after two saints, Saint this and Saint that. They were tiny things. They followed me all over the neighborhood and they were wonderful animals. But one time when the javelina got about two and a half feet long and about two feet high, a great big German police dog picked a fight with my javelina and the javelina gave him an awful good whipping and cut him up with his tusks. So my mother and father made me give him to the Brackenridge Zoo. But they were wonderful animals.

Were you ever caught doing something you weren't supposed to be doing?

Yes. I was at Hawthorne Junior School and there used to be an old lady,

Maury's father with two baby javelinas.

When you were growing up, did you play on the river?

Not much in the downtown river because it was dirty and full of old tires and junk and it was ugly and dangerous. Harry Drought, who was head of the Work Progress Administration, Robert Hugman, the architect, members of the Conservation Society, and my father got Mrs. Roosevelt to talk to President Roosevelt and then the river was fixed up. I remember going to the river at Brackenridge Park all the time because I lived next to Brackenridge Park. I also went down by the missions south of town and went to the river there.

How did you entertain yourself?

I came from a family, particularly my father, who knew a lot of interesting people all over the world. Washington, San Antonio, California, New York— some of the great writers and musicians and politicians. We would go to their homes or they would come to our home so I guess how I'd entertain myself was listening to people.

We used to go every Sunday to my grandmother's house at what was called Sunshine Ranch. All the relatives would come and there would be a hundred and fifty of them. I now have over three hundred cousins in San Antonio. My father was the youngest of eleven children.

Did your father take you hunting?

I never hunted. My father encouraged me not to hunt, not to kill animals, and I never did. He was a good historian. He wrote two books which had history in them and knew a lot about Texas history. I think I do too because of him. He was mayor and congressman, and I saw a lot of important people and had some exciting times. I did things like that instead of hunting.

Maury's father, Maury Maverick, Sr.

30

Politician Maury, Sr. campaigning.

Did you get to spend much time with him since he was so busy as mayor?

He paid a lot of attention to me. We went a lot of places together. He died very young. He was fifty-eight and a half and had a hard political life. When he was mayor, there was a riot. A mob came to Municipal Auditorium to keep a woman, a Communist, from talking. She weighed about ninety-seven pounds and couldn't hurt a flea. She had been putting up picket lines on the west side because Mexican-Americans were making about seventeen cents an hour in depression days, and were pretty close to starving to death. She did some brave things, so my father got caught up in the riot, fighting for her right to speak. That was the end of his political life. When he was in the Congress, before he was mayor, he was a lieutenant to President Franklin Roosevelt and the only congressman in the whole entire body who voted for the anti-lynching law. In the old days they would lynch black people and get away with it. My father lived a very controversial life and I was part of that as a child.

Maury, Sr., with President Franklin D. Roosevelt.

Do you remember that riot?

Yes. I was about fifteen. The police had to carry me away. I saw some of it. The mob came out to my grandmother's house and threw rocks in the windows and we had to have a police escort for my sister, mother and father for a week to keep from getting killed. It was a very terrible experience.

Did your family celebrate Texas Independence?

Sure. My great-grandfather signed the Texas Declaration of Independence. He was in the Alamo when he was elected to Washington-on-the-Brazos and he signed it there so I knew something about it.

When you were growing up, what was the Alamo like?

It was pretty much like it is now. When I was your age my father would

Maury's father at the Spanish Governor's Palace.

take me there and he would tell me both sides of the Alamo story. The Mexicans were brave too. You always hear one side. We Texans were not always right. Some of the defenders of the Alamo had slaves in there. They wanted liberty for themselves, but they had black slaves in there who were denied liberty. And that was bad. The Mexicans were bad because they were telling us how to pray, what religion to belong to, but we were bad because we had black slaves. When the battle of the Alamo was over, Santa Anna let the slaves escape and go to Mexico.

Did you have a particular favorite place in San Antonio?

I used to go to a lot of historical places when I was your age. My father and I would play the alphabet. He'd say, "With A, think of places to go to and talk about history." That would force me to think about A. A for Alamo, A for aquifer, A for aqueduct. There is a Spanish aqueduct south of San Antonio. It is one of the few aqueducts in this part of the world. It runs over a river. You will find it near Mission Espada.

We would go down there and other places. My father would act out different historical roles, and we would have good times. That's what I liked doing during those years.

When you were growing up, did you have an idol that you looked up to?

I thought Franklin Roosevelt was a great man. When the depression came, he came on the radio and said the only thing we had to fear was fear itself. It was a time in American life when we helped each other and did creative things. Here in San Antonio, like all over America, artists and musicians were hungry and so

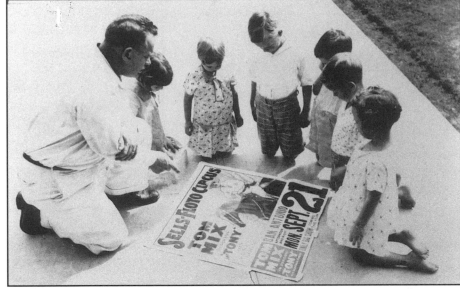

Maury, Sr., with children during the depression.

they got them into the WPA. Eleanor Roosevelt was a great friend of the black people and all the poor people. She was, and remains, my favorite First Lady in the history of the country. Magnificent woman.

I met her several times at the White House. Then while she was visiting the troops during World War II, I was a young lieutenant in New Zealand, and I called out her name. All the prime ministers and generals and admirals were standing there in Wellington, New Zealand, and she dropped all the big shots and spent about ten minutes with me and some sergeants. She was very nice to people who were not powerful or rich

and she would be very courteous. I used to correspond with her up to about six months before she died and I loved her.

Most kids want to be firemen or policemen when they grow up. Did you have any career dreams when you were our age?

Officially I was an old man in January 1986, when I turned sixty-five, and I still haven't figured out what I want to be. Even as a child I never had any wild dreams about being anything in particular. I have been a lawyer for thirty-five years, and for the last ten years I have been a newspaper writer, and today I do

33

The Works Progress Administration

The Works Progress Administration was part of the first "hundred days" of the Franklin D. Roosevelt administration. Directed by Harry Hopkins, the WPA spent billions of dollars on reforestation, rural electrification, water and sewage plants, flood control and school buildings. The WPA employed artists to decorate public buildings, write state and regional guides and perform in the federal theater. In 1939, the WPA began work on the San Antonio Riverwalk as part of a flood control and beautification project.

both. I was a civil rights lawyer for many years. I represented a black man named Sporty Harvey from San Antonio. A few years ago it was a crime in Texas to let a black man have a boxing match with a white man. I am the lawyer who took it to court so that a black man would have a right to make a living. Sporty was a good fellow. He took me to the first integrated restaurant where I had ever

eaten with black people in Texas. I was scared that I was going to be beaten up. Looking back on it, wasn't that silly? They were nice to me. Sporty had a sixth grade education but that black man taught me something.

During the Vietnam War, I represented more conscientious objectors than any lawyer in Texas. The Vietnam War was very unpopular, unlike World War II which I was in. There were a lot of young people who didn't think they ought to go to war in Vietnam and kill those people over there, where they were having their own revolution and wanted to have their own country. So young Americans came to see me to keep from going to war, and I represented them for eight years.

It was a very unfair war, the Vietnam War, because of who was drafted. We would put a cross on every house in San Antonio when a person would get killed and his body brought back. Over on the West Side of San Antonio where the Mexican Americans lived, there was a whole sea of crosses and on the north side where the wealthy Anglos lived there were very few crosses. So I came to conclude, unlike most liberals, that I am for an honest draft. One Anglo, one Mexican, one black. Fifty-fifty. No sweetheart deals because your skin is white or you are rich. Everybody dies equally.

34

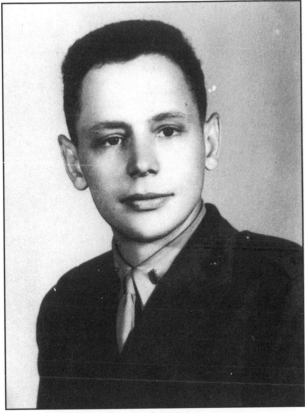

Maury, Jr., as a Marine Lieutenant.

Was your father being in politics what got you into law?

My father was a lawyer and I didn't know what else to do. Like everybody I came back from the war and had to do something, so I went to law school. I like the law pretty good, although I think it has gotten a little cold-blooded. A lot of these young lawyers refrain from taking up controversial civil liberties and civil rights cases. Too many of them think of nothing but the money.

I believe in the practice of law where you don't have to haggle over money all the time. I believe in the type of government such as they have in Sweden, for example. Accountable. A form of democratic socialism mixed with capitalism. People in Sweden are not as rich as they are in this country but neither are there as many poor people. I lived in New Zealand once, and it was a fair-minded country.

Maybe I would go into journalism completely if I had to do it over again. But that would be as bad because you could be working for a newspaper you didn't like, and as a lawyer you have a measure of independence. At least you are your own boss and you can pretty much do whatever you want.

I had some hard times as a lawyer. Once I represented the alleged head of the Communist Party in Texas. The police came into the man's house and took his books away from him. The police were the ones who were seditious. I don't care if a person is Ku Klux Klan, or Communist, or Jew, or Baptist, or conservative, or reactionary, or rich, or poor, I don't think the police should break into a person's house and get his reading material. I took that Communist case to the U.S. Supreme Court and won unanimously and the decision was rendered by a conservative Republican judge.

Nakäi Breen

Nakäi Breen, a Cherokee, has spent much of her life among the Kickapoos. Long concerned with Native American causes, Breen addressed a joint session of the United States Congress and was instrumental in helping the Kickapoos gain their reservation in Texas. Nakäi, who lives in Brackettville with her husband, painter Bud Breen, is still devoted to the Kickapoos.

Nakäi Breen

You are Cherokee?

I am Cherokee. I'm not Kickapoo. My tribe is the first civilized tribe. We took to the white man's ways very early. We were the first Indians to have an alphabet. We were the first to have a newspaper. We are altogether different from the other tribes.

Did you come to Eagle Pass when you were little?

I came to Eagle Pass when I was seven. I don't remember at what age I went to school, but I remember being baptized. I was nine years old. I was twelve when I first found my grandmother.

Tell us something about your life before you were twelve.

I had no life before I was twelve. I was looking for a grandmother and then I found a grandmother I could keep with me. I took her home and I told her she would suffer no more. We call the elders grandfathers and grandmothers out of respect. Even though they are not relatives by blood, they are relatives of respect. I brought my grandmother home and told her that as long as the Great Mystery would give me bread and sunshine every day, she would suffer no more because people that are old, if they are begging for a cup of coffee, they don't have anybody.

About five years ago, my grandmother died at the age of a hundred and three. They brought her back to me before she got sick. And she started to touch me and she told me, "I have had but one true granddaughter and that is you. I have asked the Great Mystery to take me. I am ready, now that you are a woman and have children of your own." That very day she went back and she had a stroke and for about a year and a half she kept asking for me and I never went to see her. I did not want to see her in that condition, and have it be in my mind the rest of my life. The way I see her is the way I saw her before she was sick.

When I met my grandmother the first time, she gave me my first necklace. I got my first Kickapoo dress and my first moccasins and I got part of her medicine but I cannot use it because I am not Kickapoo. I use my own. She gave me a Kickapoo name, Nakia or Nakiaka, which means "the bark that protects the tree." It's almost like mine, Nakäi. I had many a good time with her. Many a good time. When she died, everything died.

She has come to me in my dreams many times and she has told me many a thing that I didn't know before. I had forgotten how to make baskets and she taught me again. I had forgotten how to make pottery and she taught me and now I know.

What made you go look for her?

I was going to school and I saw it, that she was begging.

And you knew?

I knew that she didn't have anybody. I am a dreamer. I dream it and I see it. I am an Indian doctor. Many amazing things have happened to me. I asked a Comanche Indian doctor, "Why do I dream myself all the time as a kid?" He said because I had not found myself yet. I was lost all the time. That was the reason I was looking for a grandmother.

She loved me very much. She'd tell me about the way of life, the do's and don'ts. My biggest enjoyment was when she used to bring me pumpkin candy that she made. Or when she boiled sugar until it turned brown and put pecans in it. She used to tell me stories. She taught me how to speak English. Never was I sad after I met her. When she died five years ago I lost everything.

You weren't connected to any Kickapoos before that?

I didn't even know Kickapoos existed, and they had been there for more than 150 years. The city people called them squatters. How can one be a squatter in one's own land? They were recognized in Oklahoma as Kickapoo, but never in Texas were they accepted. I worked with them but I was not raised with them.

Where did you go to school?

In Eagle Pass. I walked to school every day. When I woke up in the morning, I washed up and went to school. On the weekend, I baby sat, cleaned yards, chopped wood, raked yards, did errands, and I asked for a dime or a quarter. A quarter was a lot of money. I could buy five bubble gums with a penny. I made that money for my grandmother, and I bought her flour, sugar, whatever.

The Kickapoos

The Kickapoo Indians are a unique group because of dual citizenship in Texas (U.S.) and Mexico. The name Kickapoo comes from Kiwigapawa which means "he moves about, standing now here, now there."

They were first encountered in Wisconsin around the late 17th century and were known for their fierce fighting. By 1839 some had begun to settle south of the Rio Grande and by 1850 members of the tribe were formally recognized as colonists by the government of Mexico.

They are one of the few Indian tribes in North America still living much as they did more than a century ago. Some of the tribe are trilingual, speaking English, Spanish, and Kickapoo. All of them speak their native Kickapoo tongue.

Wickiups

Most of the dwellings, called wickiups, belong to the women, who build the houses and make all of the mats that cover the floor. Any adult woman may build and own a Kickapoo house, with permission from the chief if she is building for the first time. If she leaves the village and does not pass her house on to a relative, she must dismantle her house in the compound and leave it clear for someone else.

When you were in school, what was the attitude of the other children toward you?

There was an Apache from Arizona or New Mexico. They called him Chief, and they always teased him. Not the children. It was the teachers who teased him. We were the only Indians there. I was forever in the wastebasket. I'd do something wrong and the teacher would stick me in the wastebasket.

At first we were put in the hall because we couldn't speak English or Spanish. Then we were put with Mexican-American kids. I used to come home and tell my father I could speak English. I would sing, "A hunting we will go, a hunting we will go, we catch a mug and put him in a lock, and lady, lady, go." I sang it like that and the teacher never corrected me. My father went there and said, "You teach the Spanish-speaking kids with flash cards, why not my kids?" So, we learned like that.

How did you go to Mexico?

I would go with my grandmother. We would walk across and go by bus about a hundred and thirty miles. Other times we went in a pickup truck and sat in the back. I remember the beauty of the huts in the morning, the smoke deep with smells. The mountains so majestic, so beautiful. The pecan trees, the river. It was a paradise. One time I got real sick, but my grandmother cured me. I didn't want to die over there. I wanted to be in my country if anything happened.

Is Kickapoo life different in Mexico than it is here?

Yes, it is. By far. They farm there. They have cattle. The Mexican government gives them a cow and a bull. They plant corn. Some they sell, some they keep. They collect peppers from the mountains. They don't eat them. They sell them. Bread is a luxury to them. They eat it at every hour, with mayonnaise, or mustard, or catsup, or honey.

Camp bread they make in a Dutch oven. They use a lot of wheat flour and a lot of corn meal. It rises. It's really fluffy, not a tortilla. They cook a lot with bear grease. In January they start hunting for the deer and the bear.

The deer is sacred and is for ceremony. The bear is like the buffalo was for the Plains Indians. They dry the meat. They pound the meat and make it real fine. They take a pinch of that and put it in the gravy or the corn or rice. They eat a lot of rice.

The Kickapoo women never tan the bear's hide. The Comanche and the Kiowa do not eat bear meat. I am a Kiowa only by adoption, not by birth. I eat the bear, but it makes me sick. I never ate fish until about ten years ago. Squash. Pumpkins. My baby goes to one of the clans and he cannot have cantaloupe, watermelon, peaches, apricots, squash, or corn until after the ceremonial dances.

I asked for this baby. This baby was sent to the hospital in Eagle Pass and then to San Antonio because he was severely dehydrated and was five days without eating. For two weeks he was in intensive care. I said, "Let me take him for six months. If he dies I will be at ease that I tried. But if I can get his health back, maybe I will give him back to the mother."

For a month I stayed up until three and then my husband would get up because the baby was so weak we had to feed him with an eyedropper. When he got well, the mother said, "I want you to raise him for me because this baby was dead and you gave him life, so I cannot take him anymore." This is because of their beliefs. When he was six months old I told his mother, "I want this baby to be baptized the Kickapoo way." They baptized the baby. I love this baby and I will never deny him that he is a Kickapoo. I will never deny who the mother is.

The children that go up north with migrant workers go to school. They are accepted; in Eagle Pass they are not accepted. The problem is that in the north they are in one place one month and another place another month. Who's going to learn like that?

When I was twelve there was no need for a reservation in Texas. When they needed surgery they went into Mexico or Oklahoma, but never in Eagle Pass. I am better not to see them, because how can I see a wounded person and not help them. The Kickapoos are dying little by little.

Is that how you got involved in getting a reservation in Texas for the Kickapoo?

When the legalities began—going to Washington, getting them land, the status of citizenship, Indian Health Services—I was appointed as their official representative, first by the Kickapoo leaders of Eagle Pass, second by Senator John Tower, then Kykendall the Indian attorney, and then the Oklahoma Kickapoo. I spoke nothing against our country, nothing against our flag, nothing against the state. Everything was to benefit the Kickapoo. They were a tribe here in the United States and they didn't have the right to anything, not even to educate their children. I think that if children do not have religion, number one, and schooling, number two, we are nothing.

STATEMENT OF NAKÄI BREEN BEFORE THE INTERIOR AND INSULAR AFFAIRS COMMITTEE, U.S. HOUSE OF REPRESENTATIVES, WASHINGTON, D.C., OCTOBER 30, 1981.

Distinguished members of Congress, Ladies and Gentlemen. My name is Nakäi Breen. I have come here to hold council with you all hoping that I can reach your minds and touch your hearts. I am here on behalf of the Traditional Kickapoo Band of American Indians that reside by the banks of the Rio Grande in the city of Eagle Pass, County of Maverick and the State of Texas. I have known and represented this proud band of Kickapoo officially and unofficially since the age of 12 years old. I have traveled many paths and trails trying to find new channels to help this people and put a stop to all the suffering and injustice that are done to them daily. It seemed that no one even cared whether they suffered or not, or maybe nobody was aware of what was going on. These people are peaceloving and very close to nature and at one time they owned millions of acres of land, but they gave it up or were forced to give it up, and the Great Migration started. They were looking for a place that they could hold tight to their religion and culture. Now they do not have a handful of Mother Earth to call their own in their native country. Our country is known to justify the unjust and a great gift the American people enjoy is even stated in our Constitution: Freedom of Religion. Is it wrong to worship and believe the way one was brought up to believe since time began? Isn't it the same Great Mystery in the heavens that everybody looks up to for guidance and protection? Our religion is like our flag, we live and die for both with honor. We are the creation of the Great Mystery. We, too, feel cold and hunger. Our hearts beat warm inside us, just like any other human being. Even though our lodges sit on different hills and our fires burn different from yours, we still feel like anybody else. These people have lived around Eagle Pass for more than 150 years. Their loved ones are buried there. But now with all the beautifying America, our huts are an eyesore to the public.

When the Great Mystery put a handful of seeds in His hand to sow the face of Mother Earth, flowers of all beautiful colors came up. It was the red flowers, however, that grew in abundance in America. In later snows, seeds of brown came in, seeds of white, seeds of black, and eventually all the colors mixed and smothered out the red flowers. All these flowers, if they are not satisfied or appreciate this beautiful soil, they can always go back to their motherland. But the red flowers, where can they go?

We need citizenship to take part of the benefits that everybody takes part of, such as old age pension. For the longest while, we thought we were American citizens. The elders do not understand the civilized world way, that there is an international boundary. They still believe the Great Mystery created a river to drink out of and bathe and cook with and cross when we need to. They do not understand why there is so much land with a fence around it and nobody lives there. They ask who sold it. They believe the Great Mystery created it for everybody.

We need health services because we have a lot of children and elders that need medical attention, but do not have that talking paper, so-called money. When we are put in the hospital, we are put in isolation and go through the hassle that money is being wasted on us. When our loved ones die, we stand in the corridors of the funeral homes until it is time to go to the funeral. In the cemetery, a bull-dozer covers the grave, leaving it with no trace of the hole and we can never put a marker on it. The children are so discriminated against inside the classroom as well as outside that they are eventually pressured to drop out.

Let us forget the old Indian wars and forget about preserving artifacts that make history, and see history living among this unique band of Traditional American Indians. In your hearts I rest my plea. May you always have a spark of sunshine in your hearts.

With sound mind and good medicine.

NAKÄI BREEN

How can one communicate with the rest of the world if you don't even know how to speak? How can one fear the Great Mystery above if you don't have religion? Those are the two main things one should have. Those two things make us better people, better citizens and better understood. That is my way of thinking.

I wrote thousands of letters. I got involved and there was no easy way to get out. I didn't have an education to help me fight, but I have a mouth so that I could talk. Anyone can read the testimony that I gave in Washington and see what I asked for. I asked for Indian Health Services, citizenship, and a piece of land. The Kickapoo said, "Just tell them to leave us a path from Mexico to here." I asked for a spot on the face of Mother Earth. I thank the Great Mystery that my dream has come true.

The day the final payment was made on the land, I said, "Today is Kickapoo day." The day they did the citizenship was flag day. If I had known what was going to happen I would have bought a little American flag and given it to every Kickapoo who was given citizenship. They put the Kickapoo citizenship papers in a sack and threw them on the table and let each one pick up their own. You know what they said? "We're proud you are American citizens; now you can vote. I will be expecting

Nakäi and Indian Delegation on the steps of the Capitol with Congressman Abraham Kazin of Laredo.

your vote." Right is right, and wrong is wrong.

Where did you get this sense of right and wrong?

From seeing. From working. From the everyday things. Why should we have a band of Indians that are a part of America with land in Mexico when here they're not even citizens. They gave up thirteen million acres in Wisconsin and Illinois. They don't want the kids to be educated in Spanish. They say, "We're in the United States and we want our kids to learn English." I had four kids in the service. I had three in Vietnam. This is my country and that's all I have. People say, "Let's beautify America." America is beautiful. Let's beautify the people.

There is not one color of the seeds that our Great Mystery planted on the face of Mother Earth that has not walked through that front door and been accepted here. They're all the same. I had never met a black person until I came to Brackettville. I had seen them in movies but it was like a fairy tale. Then in 1959, an old black man came from Houston to bring two paper sacks of clothing for the Indians. I said, "Grandfather, you're welcome in my house." Tears started flowing and he said, "This is the first time somebody has called me grandfather out of respect."

I am a Christian, the Christian way, and I have my Indian religion the Indian

Nakäi with Maketeonenodua and Congressman Kazin of Laredo.

way. One does not infringe on the other. I use both of them. Our Great Mystery represents God. Our sacred pipe is our sacred book, like the Bible. So there's no difference. A lady said, "Indians are pagans, they worship idols." I don't worship idols. I worship His creation because He's the one that created the tree, and the tree gives me fruit and gives me fuel and gives me clothing. The herbs give me medicine and food.

How long have you been married?

I have been married thirty-seven years to Bud Breen, a western artist. We had a lot of experiences living on

46

ranches. Life was beautiful. I was always more like a tomboy. If there is anything in a man's line, I can do it. I work on horseback. I know everything about cattle. How to dehorn, drench, vaccinate, castrate, brand, cut wood, work fences.

On the woman line I'm a mother, I'm a wife. I'm the owner of my home even though my husband bought it. It belongs to me because I know what goes where. The children are my kids because I am their mother. That is the Indian way. In the Indian life the husband, when he dies, is dead. The mother, when she dies, is only asleep because she has an obligation to take care of her kids until she gathers them and puts them down on the stomach of Mother Earth. As long as her children are alive, she is obligated to them. The children are not obligated to her. They are not responsible for our faults or our doings, but we are responsible for them.

My home is made mostly out of secondhand things but is a very loving home. My children were raised to love each other and to be happy with just what we had. If we don't buy them things, it is not because we don't want to.

Did you know when you were little that you had medicine?

I started curing when I was about seven or eight years old. I told my grandmother these things that I would see, and all these things that happened to me. She took me and did something to me, and from that day I could do certain things.

Were you born to the medicine way?

When one is born in the medicine, one is born with all the aspects of medicine. When medicine is passed down, it's only one kind of medicine, like the kind that smokes people, the one that heals with herbs, the one that is a seer or the one that can predict. But when one is born with the medicine, one has both medicines, the good and the bad. It is up to the person to take whichever they want.

They tell my children, "Your mother howls at the moon. Your mother throws raw meat at the fire." The Indian way, we don't know the Devil because we are the ones that make the Devil. If I wanted to do the bad, I could never have married and had children. I could never have lived with people; I'd have to live by myself. I cannot make witchcraft. I either serve one medicine or the other.

Can you go without your medicine?

I need my medicine, not for the people, but for myself. I see the world now like everybody sees the world. Dirty, poor people came to me and I took them in, sat them at my table. Now

I see that they're dirty because they want to be dirty. Those things I never saw.

Now I see through the eyes of a human. Before I saw through the eyes of an Indian. I had pity on everybody. I picked up people on the highway and brought them here and gave them a bowl of beans. How do you know if this man is bumming a ride from California to San Antonio because his mother is dead and there is only one way he can get there? To be on the road for four or five days he had to be dirty. Who are they to say he is the scum of the ground? Can they walk his path to know?

What do you look forward to?

There's nothing in life I have not asked for and received. The things that I looked for took many years. I suffered so much, looking, searching. But He gave me the pleasure of knowing them. What I looked so hard to touch, I touched it, even if it was just a wisp.

What do you hope for the Kickapoo?

I hope now that they are trying to improve their conditions, that they do not lose the way and the traditions of the Kickapoo. You can modernize yourself, but in here you can be an Indian the rest of your life. I like the good stuff but I can always go back to the Indian life because that's the way I was born. I have found that the Kickapoos have a heart; it beats and it is as warm as mine.

Stanley Marcus

Stanley Marcus was born in Dallas into a family of merchants. His first job was in his father's store and he eventually became chairman and chief executive of the internationally recognized Neiman-Marcus. In addition to his work with the store, he has been a thoughtful art collector, an outspoken citizen and a leader in the civic and cultural life of his community.

When I Was Just Your Age

50

Stanley Marcus

I understand you spent a lot of time in the store when you were growing up. How did you spend your time?

I guess my earliest experience is when I was two years old. I used to go into the ladies' alteration room and play with boxes that I mounted on thread spools. I made my own toys. Subsequently, when I was seven, eight, nine years old, I used to work at the store on Saturdays and holidays, sometimes in the summer, doing various jobs ranging from carrying supplies from the basement to the selling floor, to running cash. At that time, change was made at a central cashier and if a customer came in with a $20 bill, I had to take the money to the cashier and then bring the change back to the salesperson. Those are my earliest childhood experiences in the store.

You talk about making toys out of boxes and spools, can you remember any of your other childhood toys?

Yes, I used to play with blocks. There were wooden blocks and cast stone blocks, as I recall. They came in a wide variety of shapes and colors. I made buildings. I think that blocks were the most interesting toy that I played with. I also enjoyed playing with electric trains, but I think the blocks were probably the most persistent toy.

In your family as a whole, were you all very close?

I had no sisters, and my brothers and I were spaced out at intervals of four years, so there wasn't a terribly big area

of closeness. I think whenever you put brothers in the business, the same thing with sisters, you set up some internal rivalry. Parents have to be careful in raising children to avoid setting up situations that create tensions, misunderstandings, greed. The best possible thing is to keep them in different lines of endeavor rather than the same.

In your book, you said that you all gave jobs in your store to different people in the family. Did that have anything to do with being immigrants?

I think this was probably characteristic of some of the older Jewish families who felt a sense of responsibility for any relatives. When a relative came over from the old country or someone moved into the city, members of the family who were doing well gave them a helping hand, gave them a job. The store was always regarded as a place where anybody could work without a lot of experience. As a result, a number of members of the family were given jobs in the store. If you were a member of the family, you had a job, and it was very difficult to get rid of them.

Did a lot of your mental life revolve around the store?

There isn't any doubt of that. It became a standard topic of conversation. "How were things at the store today?"

Stanley, on the right, with his mother and brother.

The Neiman-Marcus store at its opening.

started off the discussion. My father would tell of various incidents, people who had been in, problems he had had. My aunt, Mrs. Neiman, would talk about problems of delivery of merchandise, or things they missed sales on, or great sales they accomplished. It was bound to rub off on the children.

Did your family retain many of the customs or traditions from their native country?

Small habits, connected with religion more than anything else. My mother and father were born in this country. My mother was born in Dallas. My grandparents came from Europe. My grandmother would always save everything because she lived through a period when she didn't have anything. She saved thread, she saved string, and she'd have drawers that would be filled with balls of twine because you never knew if you were going to need it sometime. I think that was distinctly an old world trait of those who came from poor circumstances. Today we have flea markets for those things.

I remember some stories that are very vague in my mind. One of my grandfathers slipped out of Russia in order to avoid being conscripted into the army. My grandmother told a lot of stories about coming across from Peoria,

Illinois, to Texas, in a covered wagon. I'm sorry that I missed the family yarns.

Did you have traditional dishes?

Not really. Basically it was fried chicken and watermelon. This was before hamburgers.

A lot of people we've interviewed talked about the land and the weather, but your upbringing was quite different.

I was led to believe that outdoors was bad and barren, that you were better

Stanley's father, Herbert Marcus, Sr., as a young man. 1905.

off indoors. It kept me from admiring a hill except as something you had to walk up. My father had no interest in the land.

He had no interest in the countryside. He loved trees and he loved flowers, but that was the extent of his interest in the countryside. I had a brother four years younger than me who loved the land, and his great interest was in farming and ranching. As far as I was concerned, it was a necessary evil. I had no relationship with the country at all. My wife said I was never in the country until I married.

What were some expectations of you by your family?

I think they all expected me to be the best in whatever I was doing, and anything less than that was not very satisfactory to them.

Did your parents influence you to be outspoken?

I'm not sure they encouraged me, but they didn't discourage me.

Did you ever feel that it was a risk to your business, to be outspoken about your beliefs?

I believe strongly that life without having the ability to express yourself isn't worth living. There were risks involved both for the business and for myself, and I had to take the risks, because any subject that's worth talking about is subject to disagreement and to argument. I made up my mind very early that if I was trained to be in the business, the business would have to accept me on my terms and give me freedom of expression.

Were you outspoken as a child?

I don't know. I think I was probably always in a spirit of revolt. I can't blame it on my childhood. I don't think I was a very interesting boy. I don't think I was a terribly happy boy. I've never been able to figure out why I wasn't happy. I wasn't deprived of anything. We didn't live in great luxury when I was a small child. But I couldn't wait to grow up. When I was 11, I said I was 15; when I was 15, I said I was 19; when I was 19, I said I was 26. I always wanted to be with older people, older girls, and lied about my age constantly.

I think one thing that was very influential in my childhood was the fact that my mother made me take elocution lessons, which gave me the experience of having to stand in front of an audience and speak. That, together with high school debating, gave me self-confidence in talking and became a very valuable attritbute affecting my success. I've always been able to get up and speak on my feet without any queasiness or any kind of fear.

What in your childhood influenced your ideas?

I think ideas come about through necessity. I find that if I've got a problem, I usually find an answer to it within two or three days, and very often from unexpected sources. It may come from reading a book or a magazine advertisement or listening to a symphony without distraction, and suddenly, a solution will hit me.

I learned to let it come to me. I guess what really happens is that I'm sub-consciously thinking about the problem and given enough relaxation that other stimuli begins to work on me and I come up with some answers as a result.

I think that I recognized, probably as a result of college education, that the world of ideas doesn't stop at boundary lines, and that there were good and better things that were happening in other places in the world, rather than believing that everything good and kind happened in Hillsboro, Texas, or Dallas. I've always had an international point of view from that standpoint, rather than the false premise that because it's local it's best. I've always been opposed to provincialism. In search for the best, it might take you to Turkey, it might take you to Warsaw, it might take you to Waxahachie.

How early did you become aware of this pattern?

I am not aware of when it first became evident. Maybe I've never had tough problems, or maybe my experiences provided me with enough resources that I can deal with problems, but I don't think I've ever had a problem I found unsolvable. I used another technique at times which has been very helpful. What I call a factoring sheet. I take a piece of paper and draw a line down the middle of it and I write down

Poster advertising the first "fortnight."

every reason for it and every reason against it, and then try to appraise which forces are the stronger, and make the decision on a reason factor basis.

Once I was looking for something that would increase the sales of Neiman-Marcus when business was slow in October. I was trying to find something that would attract people to want to come to town. I thought up this idea of a foreign fortnight. That was influenced by something that I saw in Sweden where a store there had organized a French week with a French fashion show and a French chef. I just had to take that idea and expand it so it covered a wide variety of cultural interests and brought it back and sold it as sort of a community undertaking. And it did just what I hoped it would do.

Have most of your solutions worked?

Yes. That doesn't mean you don't have failures. You have to realize the chance of failure in order to have a chance for victory. People who are afraid to take a chance on failure are unlikely to ever do anything great or creative because they're always worried about the consequences. I also learned that if you are going to make decisions, you had best spend your time worrying about them beforehand, and not afterwards. I rarely look back and wonder if I made the right decision. That's how you get ulcers and heart attacks, worrying about

Stanley's father, Herbert Marcus, Sr.

something that you can't do anything about. I think you worry about something as long as you can do something about it.

When did you decide that this is who you were, and this is what you wanted to be?

I didn't want to be. When I got out of college I was told what was expected of me, so I did it, and found to my surprise that I liked it. It didn't take me very long to make that determination.

Why didn't you quit?

Because my father was giving me the opportunity. My dad didn't have to start a business, he inherited the business. I think that it may be easier to speculate on something you didn't work your fingers off on, trying to get where it was. My father was quite remarkable in that he permitted me to take some gambles. Fortunately, most of them paid off. Some of them didn't, but the majority did. That convinced me that entrepreneurship consisted of taking risks. Without taking risks nothing new happens. If he had said, "No, you can't do that, it's too much of a gamble," I probably would have quit. But he encouraged me by letting me take chances. He began to have faith in my judgment at a very early age, when I was twenty-two, twenty-three.

I came into the business at a time when he was sort of strapped for manpower and he needed someone he could rely upon and here I was, a kid. The things he gave me to do I apparently did to his satisfaction and very quickly established a reputation. So I never underestimate the effects of luck.

To be lucky though, I think you have to be doing something. I don't think you'll be lucky staying in bed. You have to be doing something, you have to be looking for something. In science, big discoveries have been made in completely opposite fields. Looking for one thing you might find something else, and because you recognize it is something else, you didn't throw it away. You say, "This is interesting," and you do something about it. Henry Perkin discovered analine dyes while he was looking for bacteria. He never found the bacteria but he made a fortune and made a reputation on the fact that he discovered analine dyes. But again, he wasn't in bed reading a book. He was investigating.

There is a mystique to Neiman-Marcus. How did that happen? Was it intentional?

I think it started as a by-product. I don't think anybody starts to build a mystique. It's sort of like a snowball, it has to have some kernel of fact and once it starts moving downhill, it gathers up lots of stuff. That's what happened to the store, and happens to individuals. They build a reputation, they become both the victim and the beneficiary of this reputation. Some of it is fact, some of it is fiction.

The fact that we made this happen in Dallas is beneficial to us because if you try to do it in Chicago it wouldn't have had any news value. But in Dallas it had news value. If this had been done in Lincoln, Nebraska, it might have had news value, but nobody cared about Lincoln, Nebraska.

Texas was a place where there was already some legend. The legend of oil deals, oil money, cattle. I couldn't have consciously picked a better place. That was luck. I was here instead of being in Lincoln, Nebraska.

But it went beyond Texas. It became international.

I learned at an early date the value of making news. If you make news, you get publicity. You can't go to the paper and say, I want you to do a story about me. But if you do something that's news-worthy, they've got to write about you. So, I created this Neiman-Marcus Award for distinguished service and I brought Christian Dior on his first trip to America to Dallas to receive it, and Coco Chanel on her first trip to Texas, and Grace Kelly who was later to become Princess Grace of Monaco, because she was typical of the clean cut American look. Those things and those people made news. That added to the mystique.

Stanley with Grace Kelly

Stanley with Coco Chanel and his wife, Billie, on left.

During a disaster out in west Texas, years ago, I sent a telegram to all our customers giving them sympathy and telling them we could extend their credit for a year. I didn't stop to figure what it would cost. If I had, I wouldn't have done it. But it seemed like the right thing to do for neighbors. Well, nobody took a year to pay, but they all said, "That's the greatest store in the world." That added

to the mystique. It's doing the right thing, doing a lot of positive things that showed leadership.

The first Picasso painting exhibition ever held in Texas was in Neiman-Marcus. It wasn't held in a museum. It must have been about '47. When I was president of the museum, I fought the efforts to censor the museum. They wanted me to remove an exhibition because it had some communist artists in it. I identified it as being a painting of a fisherman. Well, I didn't see anything communist about a fisherman. I refused to do it. That added a little bit to the mystique.

You spent a lot of your life involved in arts, supporting arts, encouraging arts, did you feel a gap that you wanted to fill here in Dallas?

I think I realized that in most of the cities of the world that were well known, they had such things as museums and symphonies and operas, and that these were lacking in quality and depth in Dallas. And if you were going to have a museum it should be a good one, not a poor one. If you're going to have music, it should be good music and not poor music.

You've always had this image or this idea of Dallas; did you feel this as a child?

As a student going way to college in 1921, I went to Amherst in Massachusetts and nobody knew where Texas was, much less Dallas, and had no idea what Neiman-Marcus was about. They all came from Eastern prep schools and they were full of that. One of the things that I felt very keenly was this lack of being in the know and part of something that was famous and well-known. I made up my mind that I was going to try to make the place I came from well-known. Subsequently, when I came out of college, I did some things that helped contribute to making Dallas a well-known city.

Dallas today is a major, major city and I think in another fifty years Dallas will have five or six million people. It doesn't mean it's going to be a better place. Maybe not a worse place. There are a lot of advantages to living in the city. Music, theatre never came out of the country. They only came out of the city where you had enough people together. Good music, good art, good education.

But you pay a price for it. You pay a price for it in lack of intimacy.

Often in families success doesn't pass from generation to generation, but it has in yours. What do you think are factors that contribute to that?

Luck. We know hundreds of companies where a great man started something and then sons and daughters had no interest in it. Money spoils a lot of people. The necessity doesn't exist for being successful because they've got money and they think that money is success. Well, money isn't success. Money is what you do with it.

My father forced me into the business and fortunately, it turned out wonderfully. That's why I say it's to a large extent, luck. I can't imagine having gone into any other business now. Because he gave me an opportunity to do everything I want to do. He gave me an opportunity to travel, to gamble on merchandise and ideas.

When my son was growing up, they said, "You're not making enough effort to get him interested in the store." And I said, "I have no intention. If he wants to come to the store, fine; if he doesn't, that's fine too." I talked to him. I said, "You're a sophomore in college. You're going to have to make a decision. It's not going to be my decision. It's going to be your decision as to what you want to do.

Stanley with his son, Richard.

I'll help you get an education to be anything you want to be. If you want to be a minister, a teacher, a philosopher, an astronomer or an explorer, I'll help you with anything but one thing." He said, "What's that?" I said, "If you decide you want to be a loafer, you're going to do it on your own money and not mine. I won't support your ability to be a loafer."

He tried two or three different things. He worked on a ranch one summer down on the coast. He worked in a bank here one summer. One summer he worked in the store. I remember him coming home one night and as we were serving dinner, he lifted his plate and said, "That's Wedgwood." I said, "How did you know? We've just been using it ever since you were four years old." He said, "Because I unpacked twenty cases of it today." That summer he went to Paris to work in our foreign office. When he came back he said, "I decided I want to go into the store." I said, "That's fine. Just remember it's going to be tougher for you to be successful than if your name was Smith. People will be expecting the impossible from you. It's going to be very tough, but you're welcome, and

62

we'll do everything we can to make you happy and successful."

He came into the store and never flaunted his name or his position or abused it and he became very, very successful.

Do you think that that attitude about usefulness and not loafing came from your father?

Yes. My father, I'm sure, would have told me the same thing. My father was a great teacher. I am tremendously indebted to him. He was a man of great quality, a man who was willing to stand by principle even when it cost him money. Most people are strong on principle as long as it's free. He had a great feeling that there was a responsibility in the family for the strong and successful to help those who were less fortunate, less able. He recognized there would be

times when one or the other of us would need help and it was up to those who had the ability and the natural capacity to respond. My parents took the job of being parents very seriously. There was that serious relationship between parent and child.

What advice would you give to a child growing up in Texas?

I've learned enough that I don't give advice unless somebody wants me to. Advice that you give gratuitously doesn't stick to anybody. I blame parents for a lot of the problems today. I think children respond to parent leadership. But it becomes more difficult when other parents aren't exercising leadership. Maybe what we need to do is to let the children out of school and put the parents in the school.

John Armstrong

John Armstrong came from Armstrong, Texas, grandson of the famous Texas Ranger John B. Armstrong, who was instrumental in the capture of the notorious gunmen King Fisher and John Wesley Hardin. An avid horsemen and fisherman, Armstrong has spent most of his life in South Texas with ranching and business interests.

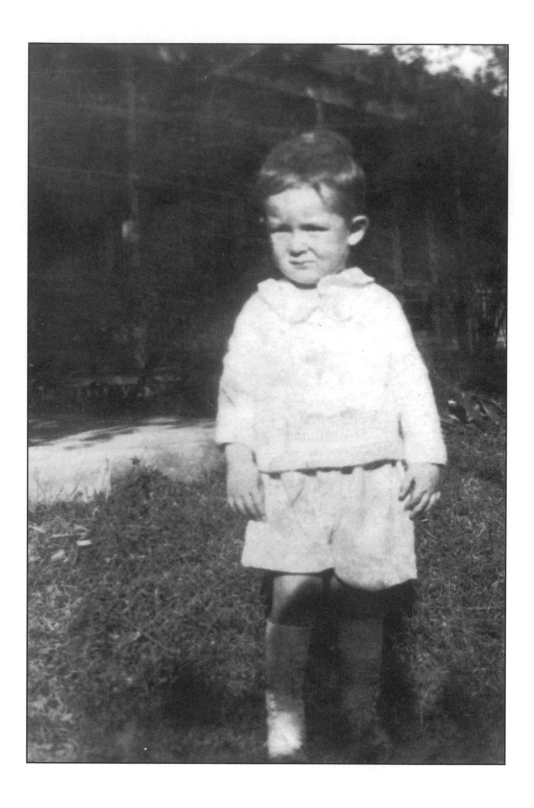

John Armstrong

What was it like where you grew up?

I was born in San Antonio, December 23, 1919, the eldest son of Charles Michael Armstrong and Lucie Tobin Carr. But I grew up at the Armstrong Ranch, which is next to the King Ranch. While it's a 50,000 acre ranch I always stated

that apologetically when I was younger because the King Ranch and the Kenedy Ranch seemed so big by comparison.

The ranch house was two miles east of the railroad station known as Armstrong. Our only contact with

Armstrong, until I was twenty years old, was the railroad. In my earliest youth, when we traveled to Kingsville or to Brownsville or points in between, we did it almost entirely on the train. Because it wasn't until later on that the Model T's came in and we began to learn how to drive them in the sand. They only had two wheel drive. It was a major expedition in those early years to drive in one of those old cars from Armstrong to Kingsville. But it was even more of an expedition when my grandfather first went there and had to do it with mules or horses pulling a wagon or carriage.

Early transportation on the ranch.

When we came from San Antonio, we got in a railroad Pullman and slept overnight, got up an hour before daylight, carrying a lantern of some kind, got off the train while the train took water (steam engine you see), and then they'd have what we called an ambulance—Army surplus equipment—and a team of mules or horses pulling it. We'd

get in that and take that two mile ride in the dark over to the headquarters. Lots of times it was still dark when we'd get there.

As a child, what were your daily chores?

You'll have to define when I stopped being a child because, as I got older, my chores and what I had to do was different, outside of the daily routine of getting dressed and going to school through the Calvert School System. My mother taught me through about the third grade,

John's mother.

and I used up a good bit of each day doing that.

As I got older I had other responsibilities. When we were out of school, I used to go help the men on all kinds of jobs that they did, like cutting wood, because that's the only kind of fire we had in those days—we used a wood stove. I learned how to use an axe. We used to haul the wood on a wagon with a team of mules or horses. When I was seven I was driving a Model T Ford, and I used to go the two miles to the Armstrong railroad station and get the mail.

Then as I got older, I learned how to milk the cows. The year that I was eleven, I milked the cows and provided the milk for the house, and I ran some of the milk through a separator each day to separate out the cream. The most interesting activity that I became involved in very early in my life was riding horseback and learning how to gentle foals, and to brand and that kind of thing. That was my keenest and most consuming

John with his father.

interest then and has continued to be throughout my life.

John on the shooting range.

By the time I was eleven years old, I was a pretty good cowboy and could do just about anything that you'd expect a cowboy to do, like rope and train a horse. I had a good teacher, my father. He was outstanding. Then I also had some other people that he thought were real good that I learned a lot from.

What were some of the games you played and who were your playmates?

I learned how to shoot when I was very young and got a lot of pleasure out of it, as did my two brothers who were my only playmates.

Once in a while, guests the age of our parents would come, and they'd bring their children with them. We looked forward to that because it was a great experience to have new faces on the scene. That didn't happen much except in the summertime and during the hunting season.

We learned how to play ping-pong because my mother was good at that. We had a game called beanbags. A board with different size holes in it. My mother would always make us put up a nickel for each game, winner take all. We played croquet. We learned how to play poker because our father wanted us to.

Friends come to visit. John is third from right.

Some people might think that would not be the right thing to teach a little child, but when people came to visit us, we'd always have big poker games (penny ante) as part of the activities. There wasn't any tennis court to play on, and we didn't learn how to play baseball or football like most kids do at that age because there weren't enough of us to do it.

John Hill, who was nineteen, came to tutor us by the time all three of us were ready for a more formal school situation. I was nine years old. All of us went to school with the same tutor at the same time. My brothers, Charles and Tobin, were in the same grade of the Calvert School System even though there was a one-and-a-half year spread in their ages.

After school we'd play a game called "antie over." What we did was to make a ball out of string and then sew a buckskin cover on it. We made it ourselves. Then two would get on one side and two on the other side of a building. First, you'd say "antie." They'd call "over." You'd throw the ball over the roof and if somebody caught it before it hit the ground, he could come around the end. You listened for him to come around, watching for him, because if he got on that side he'd throw the ball at you. If he hit you, you were out. It ended up there was only one player left. He was the

winner. We used to have a lot of fun doing that.

Was there much time for music and other spare time activities?

My mother played the piano, and every Sunday she would conduct church services around it and we'd sing hymns. That was the beginning of our learning how to sing. All three of us could sing pretty well, and we enjoyed it. We memorized the words to songs off phonograph records, like Jimmy Rogers' songs, the "TB Blues," and "T for Texas," and other songs I still sing. I learned Spanish and English simultaneously and I learned how to sing Mexican songs and harmonize with the cowhands. A great many of the songs I learned before I left Armstrong I can still remember and still sing. I didn't learn how to play an instrument until I started to school in San Antonio.

What instrument did you learn to play?

I learned how to play the guitar. My mother took me to Sears, Roebuck, and bought a guitar for me for five dollars which included ten lessons. I never had any more lessons after that. But I used to play and watch other people play, and I'd get them to show me how to do certain things, so a lot of the things that I now do with a guitar I picked up from people I enjoyed listening to.

to that, we had a ranch that was profitable, with difficult times during those years. I loved the land almost like it belonged to me, though my father was only one of five brothers and sisters, and he owned one-fifth interest.

So, I guess that love of the land and family and the traditions that we wanted to live up to; the fact that our land had belonged at first to the Indians, then to the Spaniards, and from them to Mexico, to the Republic of Texas, and finally, as a

Your life does seem happy back then, happier than a lot of people's now. How do you explain that?

I think we were fortunate to be isolated the way we were. We were shielded from a great deal of the strife and hardship of a lot of people concentrated in big cities and that sort of thing that produces so many of the economic distortions. When we were growing up, we just didn't have much contact with it because there were very few people in the area where we lived. And not so many of them even now.

What things most influenced your life, growing up?

We had a happy, close knit family and we had a lot of fun together. We had a great love for each other which has endured throughout our lives. Added

72

state of the United States; all of that history of the Civil War, the Spanish-American War, and all of those things, had some significance in the history of our ranching enterprise.

The land titles were traced back to the King of Spain. The names of the land grants were in Spanish. Like the Santa Gertrudis land grant. So the tradition of loving the land, knowing how to use it, how to take care of it and not over-graze it and to have the cattle do well on it, were drilled into me from as far back as I can remember. I loved all of that. It was the type of life that I enjoyed so much I made it a life's career. I've always been involved in land and livestock. I always will be.

What was it like to have a Texas Ranger in the family? Did it influence your ways?

You wouldn't expect somebody that died six years before I was born as having influenced me. John B. Armstrong's personality and character were so strong and he was so revered by his children that he made a profound impact on my life. I was brought up to admire and respect him and all that he had done and stood for. He was set on a pedestal as an example of someone who was an outstanding citizen, person, and father. I was constantly reminded by my father and aunts and uncles that Papa said thus, and so it was the right way to

Texas Rangers

"Texas Ranger" was applied to peace officers as early as two years after the founding of American settlement in Texas. Rangers were authorized to operate throughout the state, but wore no prescribed uniform. Their main duties were to suppress Indian and Mexican raids, outlaws, stock thieves and feuds.

John B. Armstrong, one of the most famous Texas Rangers, enlisted in Captain L.H. McNelly's Rangers in 1875. This "Special Force" operated along the Mexican border.

He also participated in the fight at Palo Alto Prairie and the Las Cuevas war. He was instrumental in the capture of desperadoes King Fisher and John Wesley Hardin. In 1882, he established the 50,000 acre Armstrong Ranch in Willacy County. He died at Armstrong, May 1, 1913.

BARBED WIRE COMES TO TEXAS

The first barbed wire factory was set up at DeKalb, Illinois, by a couple of farmers. John W. Gates, a salesman for the company, was in San Antonio in 1877 but was having no luck in selling the fencing.

"I'll tell you what, young fellow," one of the older, richer cowmen remarked. "If you can prove to me that stuff will hold a herd of mean and mangy longhorns on the prod, I'll buy the whole caboodle."

"You're called," young Gates replied. "Just meet me on the plaza out there, late tomorrow afternoon, and you'll have your proof."

A corral of cedar posts and barbed wire was built on Military Plaza and filled with as many mean-looking an assortment of longhorn steers as the cowmen could gather.

When Gates gave the signal, his hired cowboys hazed the longhorns into charging the fence. On they came at a clumsy gallop, tails up, heads down, bawling their fury. They hit the wire and bounced back, hit it again and retreated. Bewildered, badly scratched, and humiliated, they backed off and eyed the barrier, bellowing dismally.

Only five tons of barbed wire were produced in the nation three years before Gates' demonstration. Forty thousand tons were produced three years after it.

That showdown in Military Plaza in 1877 was the beginning of the end of the open range and trail herding in Texas.

do things. I felt like I knew him. He influences me to this day. It's a very high standard to have to live up to.

How about the animals you grew up with?

We had horses that were basically descended from the ponies that came from Spain. They were small, they were comfortable to ride, and they had tremendous endurance. My father introduced Thoroughbred stallions and we raised our own horses and eventually played polo on the horses we raised. I still do that.

The most interesting evolution is that of the cattle that started out being the longhorn cattle that came up from Mexico. In an effort to improve the beef

John and his sons on the polo field.

The Brahman herd.

Durham cattle. There was a tremendous interest in Brahman cattle and my father bought a herd of twenty-five Brahman cows from Mr. Al McFaddin, near Victoria. Mr. McFaddin gave what turned out to be the best looking cow in the herd to my mother.

The first thing I can remember is being kept in a wire pen at Armstrong. I would beg the cook, Willie Flores, to get me out of the pen and take me to see the Brahmans. He'd ride me on a pillow upon the pommel of the saddle and we'd go out in the pasture in front of the house to see our herd of Brahman cows.

I loved that Brahman herd. I grew up with it. We used bulls out of those cows on our Durham cows, and by the time I went away to school in 1933, our cattle had gotten to be crossbreeds of browns and blacks and reds and duns, brindles

qualities of the cattle on our ranch as well as the King Ranch, we introduced English shorthorns and Herefords. By the time I was born, most of the cattle on the Armstrong Ranch were red short-horns, but in those days we called them

The mixed herd.

and paints, many colors and types. They would fight you, too. They were very dangerous cattle with good size horns.

When I got out of school I went back to the ranch. By then the Santa Gertrudis had been recognized as a breed of cattle. We started converting our whole population to Santa Gertrudis. That's what it is now. We figured that the mineral phosphorous was lacking and was needed to make the cattle do better. That was the results of experiments done by Uncle Bob Kleberg at the King Ranch. That phosphorous supplement increased the production of our cattle by one-third. And then when we added Santa Gertrudis blood, we figured that added another third. The combination of those two things made a tremendously favorable impact on the profitability of ranching in South Texas.

What did you eat?

The main staple in our diet was frijole beans and rice, the two things that the Mexican people ate. We ate tortillas, mostly corn tortillas. We didn't eat much beef because we had to sell our cattle to make enough money to live on, and eating beef was like eating our income.

We didn't eat many vegetables. The sandy soil was too poor to grow them and we didn't have refrigerators. Someone would go to the railroad station every afternoon to get the evening mail and the provisions, the food items that were shipped from Kingsville on the train. A one hundred pound block of ice would be loaded at Kingsville in a sack with straw tied around it and it would be dropped off the evening train out of the express car. By the time it got to the house, there'd only be about 60 pounds left. It went into what we called an icebox.

We had some fruit because we had citrus down in the Rio Grande Valley, but it wasn't really a balanced diet.

John with buck.

76

We ate a lot of game during the hunting season. We lived on that. We had meat every day then. We ate the liver, the heart, the kidneys, everything that was edible. We didn't throw anything away.

How would you describe your house when you were a child?

The house in Armstrong was built in two sections. The dining room and kitchen were plastered adobe and built before the main house was attached to it. The main house was a one-story frame building, very well constructed, with very good lumber. There was a concrete porch in front of the living room and the dining room. In front of each bedroom there was a door out to a board porch. The house was built before the turn of the century, about 1890, and was very unusual because every bedroom had its own bathroom with hot and cold running water.

What kind of furniture did you have?

The furniture we had was not expensive. It was strong, attractive and comfortable. It served the purpose. It had utility. My father's office had oak furnishings. Beds were mostly four poster type that stood high off the floor. Some rooms had two beds in them.

Generally, in those early days they didn't have those nice single beds like we have now.

The only time that I remember being uncomfortable was when we'd have one of those cold spells. Of course we had to take a bath in that cold weather. The wood stove in the kitchen had a fifty gallon water tank and coils of pipe that went through the firebox. Even though it was a wood stove, we managed to have warm water to take a bath. But there was not much warm water early in the morning. There was a battle between us and our parents about getting in that tub when the water wasn't warm. And the room was cold as it could be, even when the tub was warm. That was a shivery experience.

Did you learn patience and sensitivity, or did you consider life hard?

I considered the life that I've had very happy, fun. In many ways my father and mother required us to be disciplined. They required that we wash our faces and our hands and comb our hair and button our collar for every meal. We had to put on a coat to go to supper when we had guests. But we enjoyed being together. My mother and my father were good storytellers and conversationalists. We practiced the art of entertaining ourselves and entertaining each other.

We didn't think of it as hard. We enjoyed everything we did. Except when I had to dig a hole for one of those cows that died from phosphorous deficiency. Usually she'd been dead four or five days, and you had to dig a hole right beside her. But there were no other jobs that unpleasant. Most of the things we did we made a game of it, and we looked forward to doing things together.

What is your favorite memory about growing up?

It's hard for me to identify my favorite memory because I was born into a strong current of ethical thinking, what's right and wrong, and how you should conduct yourself. I still feel a sense of obligation to live up to the standards that were set for me by Grandpa Armstrong and my parents.

There was one incident that influenced me a great deal. When I was twenty-one, my father died in an automobile accident. Losing my father was a great blow to me. I was devoted to him.

Several weeks later, Mr. Caesar Kleberg came to see me. He was a lifelong bachelor who had been best man in my parents' wedding. He lived at Norias and we'd grown up knowing him, loving him, enjoying his company, and admiring him very much. All of us did.

I was glad to see Mr. Kleberg because I was living at Armstrong by myself, and there wasn't anybody else there except the people that worked there. When I saw him drive in, I asked him to come in and have supper, looking forward to visiting with him because he was always so much fun. He said, "No, I don't have time to stay because I have other obligations, but I had something I wanted to say to you."

Then he said, "Just remember that when you get so that your work is your play, you've got it made. Goodbye." And he drove away.

That's been very valuable advice to me. I've tried to make a game out of everything I've done all my life since then. It has served me well.

Paul Baker

The son and grandson of Presbyterian ministers, Paul Baker was born in Hereford, Texas. Although he has spent most of his life in the city, as an educator and theater director, he has maintained his ties to the country. Baker has retired on a ranch in Gonzales County where he pursues his lifelong work with art because of its ability to free man's spirit.

Paul Baker

Where were you born?

I was born in the third to the last house at Twenty-five Mile Avenue, Hereford, Texas. The town was about twenty-five hundred people. It was strictly a horse-and-buggy kind of life with great ranches. Those old ranchers were marvelous, hospitable people. They served wonderful meals in a little old house out there on the prairie. The architecture wasn't much, but every now and then there was a very well-to-do rancher with a nice house.

81

What can you tell about your grandparents?

My grandfather was a Confederate veteran from Tennessee. He was a scout in the Confederate army when he was fifteen. He was also a Presbyterian minister. He was a tall, thin fellow with a hooked nose and a loud voice. They say you could hear him a mile away when he was preaching. He believed that a minister should not take money except a pounding two or three times a year. A pounding means everybody brings you a pound of flour or something. He farmed during the weekdays and preached on Sunday. He really did take care of his people. He was also very blunt.

He was a marvelous old man. I remember once when he came, the first silent movie was being shown downtown and he took us to see it.

What about your family, what were they like?

I was born into a Presbyterian minister's family. I was the youngest, with two brothers and two sisters. My father had gone to Trinity University when it was in a place called Tehuacana, and he had met my mother there, Loretta Chapman. They fell in love and got married, probably about 1892. They went to Hereford in the late 90's and he was pastor of the church.

Paul's grandfather and father.

My father had attended a very liberal seminary in Chicago. He believed in doing a lot of social work and was much loved by his community. Our house, about a mile from the church, became the community center. My sister played the piano, we all did recitations, sketches, read and told stories. We had socials and cookouts and hayrides, that sort of thing. I grew up as a vital part of the religious, entertainment and leisure time activities of the community.

I was the youngest son and when the others were gone to school, I didn't have anyone to play with. From the time I was three until I started to school my father took me with him downtown. We would harness the old sorrel to the buggy or surrey and go to town every morning and get the mail and a newspaper, the *Fort Worth Star-Telegram.* Then my daddy would visit people around town and I went with him.

He was always very proud of me and I was glad to see his friends and hear what he said and see him size up people. It was great training. I went with him on visits to the sick and to see his parishioners all over the county. I got, from a very early age, a wonderful kind of insight into people because he was a very sym-pathetic man and at the same time a very

complicated man. I think there were about five people inside my father and each of them could be quite different inside of fifteen minutes.

What age was this that you would go with your father?

From about three until I went to school at seven. We didn't go to school until we were seven in those days. When you've got that many brothers and sisters going off to school every morning, there's always a hell of a noise and getting everybody fed and

getting their clothes ready and their books together and getting off to school. I think they all walked, unless there was terrible weather. They usually walked about a mile. You didn't think anything about walking a mile. My mother was kind of an invalid; she wasn't strong. After they left, the house quieted down and I played around, went outdoors, and anything I wanted to until I went with my father to town.

What did you do for fun?

The church had marvelous socials and picnics. Everything pretty much revolved around the church or the school. I wasn't in school but one year in Hereford, but life revolved around my sisters' and brothers' schooling. There probably weren't fifteen or twenty seniors in the class, so they were all in-volved with athletics and the other social activities.

We had sketches and skits that we did. We ran and played ball, played marbles. Croquet was a big thing. They made a tennis court and started playing tennis when I was about five or six. I never got any good at it because the ground was so rough. We rode horses.

I also enjoyed discovering things. We had a large place where my father farmed, raised a garden, and raised chickens, cows, and hogs, because he didn't make enough money out of the church to live on. We all had to pitch in and do a lot of work. I was given little bantam chickens and I was anxious to see how they laid an egg. I know I spent many hours trying, but I never did see how. I was interested in watching the chickens and the cows and horses, and that sort of thing.

Were there ever any conflicts in your family?

Our family was very close knit, much like an Amish family. At night we sat around a big fire. We had a two-

84

story house, not a big house, but we had one big living room, and in the winter it was very cold and the only fire in the house was in the living room with a pot-bellied stove. My brothers and sisters were at their table in the corner working on their lessons. I played around the fire, near my mother and father. You had to live as a unit. You would freeze to death if you went off to your room.

If a visiting minister came by, and one often did come by, we had to give him one of our bedrooms. My daddy and these ministers always seemed to think that they ought to have prayer services before we went to bed. We all had to get on our knees and have a prayer. Sometimes they would get into a contest to see who could pray the longest, and go on for thirty minutes.

What childhood sicknesses were there in the family?

I don't think we had hardly any. The big sickness, of course, was about 1917 when so many people died of the flu epidemic. The doctors in the town were sick and my father was one of the few people left to take care of the sick. He never got the flu. He'd be gone all night sometimes. He'd go to some family and everybody in the family was so sick they couldn't move, and he had to stay all night and take care of them. I think different members of my family had the flu. We didn't get deathly sick with it, but a lot of other people died.

Winter in West Texas.

Was there a big difference in the seasons?

Yes. In West Texas you have a lot of hot dry winds if it happens not to rain, which it doesn't very often. From the middle of May through the summer you have scorching heat. We kept our milk cool by the windmill. They built a house under the windmill and ran a long trough inside this little house with a cover on it. You put your milk and butter in there and ran a trickle of water through it in the summer. In the winter, of course, you didn't worry about that. We had hog-killing time and cow-killing time. We lived much the way people had been living for the last two hundred years.

There was a definite winter in Hereford. When the frost came, you looked out the window and saw the whole countryside moving toward you, these tumbleweeds rolling towards you. We spent a lot of time around the fire. We had a little oil stove in the kitchen which mother cooked on, with six burners all run by a tank of oil at the end. It had a special compartment for the baking. One winter, snow was on the ground three months. Cattle were frozen or starved to death. Ranchers had to take huge sleds with a team of eight or ten horses to pull hay out to the animals.

There was one windstorm when I was about four which I will never forget. We had an iron fence. The next house

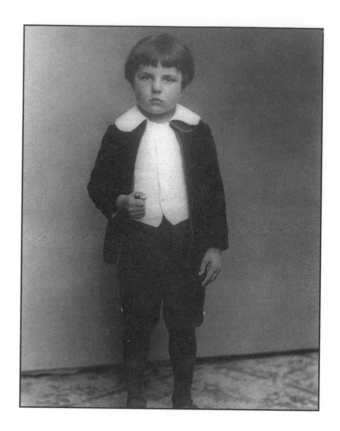

didn't have a fence, and the next house had a high wooden fence. That was where Jack, one of my best friends, lived. They had a big wooden gate to protect the house from the wind and the storms. I left my house without my family knowing it and went to see Jack. On the way the wind really got up. You know how quick it can come up. I got to Jack's and I couldn't get the gate open. I couldn't get back home. I must have been there thirty minutes before somebody discovered I was missing. Then they began to search for me in that terrible wind. When they found me I was all beat up from the blowing sand and

86

gravel, and I cried mud. That was a terrible experience for a little boy.

The windstorm sounds like a drama. What other dramatic moments do you remember?

I think one of the most touching dramas was the day my brother went away to World War I. My mother had reared the family next door, whose mother had died and left four girls and one boy. Their father was a groceryman and they were members of our church. My brother fell in love with the second daughter. I remember he courted her in his buggy and we all ran along behind it.

We had an old dog and the dog followed. That didn't make them too happy. He became engaged to her before he went to war. He knew he was going overseas as a support to the Lafayette Escadrille. He wasn't a flyer, he was an officer.

He came home before he went overseas. He was in his uniform and we all thought he looked magnificent. He was home a couple of weeks and then came time for him to go. My mother had a strong attachment to him because he was her oldest son and because for some time he was the only child. My father didn't get along with him very well, probably jealousy.

I will never forget the anguish of that goodbye. My mother was distraught. The girl was almost fainting. We all were. In those days nobody had been across Red River, much less across the ocean. You imagine demons and everything else is going to get your brother.

Did your family travel a lot?

My family didn't travel a lot. How did you travel? You mostly went by train in those days. That's the only way you could travel unless you wanted to ride a horse. Then in 1918, we bought a Model T Ford. There were other cars in town, but not very many. You started it with a crank. The faster you went the better the lights burned.

It was a good car. Since my mother was an invalid the doctor said she ought to get away from the hot sun and the wind in Hereford in the summer and we should go to the mountains in New Mexico. My father investigated the whole thing and found out that if you were going to go there you ought to carry your stuff with you because the people there didn't have a lot. He got a big trailer and we loaded it down with all kinds of stuff. The front door of the car by the driver didn't open in those days;

Paul standing by the family car.

it was solid, but the back door would open. We decided to take our chickens along with us so we built a chicken coop and put our chickens along the running board by the driver's side.

Four children, father and mother, and all the chickens, started out to Roswell, New Mexico, and up into the

mountains. At Hereford the trail was pretty good. There were tracks where they had driven wagons and in the middle there would be a big center of grass. At the New Mexico border the tracks got hazy. We went a little farther and we'd come to creeks and there weren't any bridges. We'd all get out. Sometimes a local citizen would come out and we would pay him a buck and he would pull us across with his horse.

Finally we came to the first mountains, and nothing, nothing could get that trailer up the mountain. It's hard to climb today in a car. We made a deal with some guy and left the trailer with him and we went on up into the mountains. The road went up and up and around the mountain, just wide enough for a vehicle. They had little inserts where you could stop, drive in, and wait for the other guy to pass. I thought we'd never get to the top of that mountain. We had lived on the plains all our lives, so when I looked down, I got old fast. Everybody in the family got out except my father, who always shouted when he got excited. It was really very pleasant once we got up there, but you had to get back down. Anyway, it was quite a trip in those days. That's equal to going around the world now.

At what age did you begin working?

I worked mowing lawns every summer from the time I was eight or nine until I went to college. Most of the kids in the neighborhood wouldn't do any work and I'd mow their lawns while they sat on the front porch. I must say that most of their mothers paid me and that most of the boys who sat on the front porch didn't amount to much, at least they never did hold down a regular job hardly.

I had an old hand mower, no motor on it, but it was a good Eclipse mower. I mowed nearly all the lawns in, oh, a three-block area. I didn't mind mowing the lawns so much, but I hated chopping around the edges and cutting the grass away from the curb. That like to have killed me, but I did that too.

Several summers I worked on my grandfather's ranch in west Texas, milking four cows a day and heading maize. In those days you had to go along with a knife and a horse and wagon and cut the heads off the maize and throw them in the wagon. I also picked cotton when I was about eight years old. I didn't do a lot of chopping cotton; I hated that

worse than picking it. But picking cotton was very hot. You get down on your knees in the heat and pull that sack with 100 to 150 pounds in it.

I also worked in the winter. I worked in the Safeway store as a stockboy and in the summer I worked once at Chapman Ranch, as a stock boy all summer. One summer I sold *Holland Magazine* all over Oklahoma. I had just graduated from high school.

When I graduated from college and went to graduate school, I had many intermediary jobs. I waited tables. I stoked furnaces at Yale. The first job I had when I got out of Yale was working at $12.50 per week as Technical Director for the Dallas Little Theater. You can't do very well on $12.50 but that's what I was living on. I worked there three or four months and my brother and mother thought I ought to try teaching. They got me a job teaching school in Albany, Texas, three months after the term started. I was teaching English and theater.

The day I arrived, two big football players in my senior class said, "We whipped the other guy that was ahead of you and ran him off."

I felt that I might have trouble with these two. In those days they could play a football player longer than he was supposed to play. They would sometimes change their ages so they could keep them until they were 21 or 22, and these boys were both overage and mean as they could be. One was called "Ironhead" and the other was called "Marshall More."

Paul with his sister.

There was the senior picnic. I was sponsor for the seniors, and they showed up at the picnic drunk and I called the police, and they vowed revenge. They followed me to school every morning and hurled names at me and that sort of thing. One night I walked to the movie, about three-quarters of a mile from where I lived, and they came and sat behind me and said ugly things all during the movie.

When I got out and started home, they followed me. I had one friend in town, named George, who ran a filling station. The boys accosted me again, and I told George, "I'm just going to have it out with these two guys." We went behind the filling station, and I said, "I'll fight you one at a time." While I was fighting Marshall, Ironhead picked up a rock and came up behind me and hit me in the head. They had to take me to a doctor because I was completely out. The doctor wrapped my head in a big bandage. I went to school the next morning and I had perfect discipline from then on out.

What was the most important lesson you ever learned?

I wanted to go to Yale to graduate school. I had three student friends. One was going to Chicago and two were going to Princeton. We didn't have any money. It was the peak of the depression years.

I bought an old 1919 Model T for five dollars and I renovated it. I took the head off the motor and put in new rings and new spark plugs. I took the bands off the three clutches. Forward and reverse and the brake. I refurbished and repainted the outside in garish colors. I fixed the car up with a new top. I don't know how much I spent on it but not much.

When it wouldn't start, you could jack up the back wheel and crank it. If it didn't knock you down or break your arm, it would start. In the morning when it was cold, you'd get a tea kettle of hot water and pour on the manifold.

We organized an entertainment tour on our way up to school. We stopped at various churches. They were wonderful singers and I read things and the others told jokes and stuff. We would stop and get lodging and a collection.

That car ran all the way to Chicago, New Haven, and I brought it back the following year through the Deep South. Later a man bought the car and put a saw on the back wheel and sawed wood for years with it. I was very proud of that old car. I wish I still had it.

I had to learn to take that car apart, visualize how those parts went together, how that car worked from inside out. Through trial and error and stickability I developed a real respect for working with one's hands. And the honesty it gives you. Either you get the screw on

Paul as a young man.

tight enough or else you don't. It fits or it doesn't fit. And the satisfaction of doing the job. To be able to evaluate a piece of work after it is done and to say, it's a good job, or a mediocre job, or a poor job, but I did finish.

I don't think anyone is going to amount to anything without that basic integrity and knowledge which comes only to an individual who faces a problem by himself and solves it by himself out of his own energy and with his own hands.

What influences in your life traveled from one generation to another?

My family were responsible people. They had a great feeling of service. My grandfather preached for sixty years, and never got paid for it. He thought it wasn't good that ministers, like my father, were paid.

I have the same sense of service. I felt I should stay in Texas and build a theater and do something for the people here. I had chances to go to New York and work a number of times. I didn't want to do that. I wanted to prove that there were artists down here and that we had as much talent as anywhere else. And we do.

Fannie Chism

Fannie Chism was born September 24, 1898 in Marion County where she has lived most of her life. She returned to school several times in her life and completed 12th grade when she was ninety years old. She has been active in her church, the National Association for the Advancement of Colored People, and has written and given public readings of her poetry.

Fannie Chism

What was your home like?

In them days, houses wasn't nothing to compare with what there is now. I was born in a log house, but it was in a pretty place. Most of the people were just poor people and there wasn't nothing here but farmers and that was all they did. They worked on the halves. Every once in a while you could find one who was able to rent, but most of them worked on the halves because nobody had nothing. But we made a living at it.

Working on the Halves

Before the Civil War great plantations were worked by slaves and netted the owner a large cash profit. After the war, many of the plantations were divided into smaller farms. The farms were either sold to new owners or rented to farmers called tenant farmers.

"Share cropping" or "working on the halves" was a form of tenant farming. Rather than paying cash rent for farm land, a tenant could arrange to pay a share of the farm produce. The share was negotiable but depended on whether or not the landowner furnished a house, seed, farm equipment, etc. When the tenant provided only labor, the landowner typically took half of the crop produced. The system gave families with no money a place to stay and an opportunity to share in the fruits of their labors. However, the system was subject to abuse. Some families were forced to farm unproductive land or to move if a crop failed because of insects or unfavorable weather. Families were at the mercy of landowners, who could evict them once the crop was harvested.

Your father was a farmer?

He was a farmer from South Carolina. He emigrated here after slavery and married my mother. My mother was reared in the state of Texas. I never have seen none of my daddy's people. I only saw pictures of them. We never did go there.

Fannie's father.

Do you have brothers and sisters?

I have two sisters outside of myself, two sisters and one brother that lived. But they've all passed away now, but one. I had two children and they both passed away. I'm just might near left alone, in a way.

Can you tell us what it was like growing up in Texas?

It was pretty nice in a way. There wasn't much education for black people in those days because we all had to work and we lived on the white man's places.

We didn't get to go to school until after Thanksgiving because they always had cotton and we had to stay and pick until all the cotton was out. School was always out the last of March because then we was ready for the fields. We didn't have but four or five months of school and we didn't get to go all of that. I never went to school nine months in my life. But we had good teachers what time I did go.

What kind of school did you go to?

Kellyville Elementary School. That was most all they had. They did have high school in the cities, but if you didn't have some relatives in the city, you just couldn't go to them places.

How big a school was it?

It was a big school then. Sixty or seventy scholars in one little building not much larger than this room. All of them went to that same school. For high grades they went to Jefferson to live, or they walked seven miles to Jefferson. Very few of them got any further than the tenth grade.

What was your home life like? Did you have chores?

Everybody worked at my house. We was farmers, and everyone that was big enough to work had a job to do. My daddy liked for me to cook, so I had to

cook and then go to the fields. The rest of them had to milk the cows, feed the hogs, and then go to the fields. I had to cook their dinner and take it to them.

My daddy died on the 24th day of October, 1913. I was fifteen years and one month old the day he died. We just stayed on and worked. Mama was raised on a farm and she could do her own plowing. We drilled corn, picked cotton, chopped peanuts. When we got through with that, there'd be somebody else

Fannie with her mother.

that'd have cotton to pick, or peas to pick, and we'd work there for a share. That's the way we made it. Mama never did marry no more. We stayed with her until every one of us married out, and then she turned and stayed with us. We made out all right.

Where did you go when you went to town?

We walked to Jefferson and back by sundown. Like the 19th of June was coming, or the 4th of July, and we wanted a dress or shoes, we'd walk to Jefferson. Where we traded then was a big department store owned by Mr. T. V. Rowe, and he kept a little of everything, groceries, merchandise, and all that. We'd buy whatever we was able to buy, and come back home. We'd get back just about sundown.

Did you do anything for fun while you were in town?

There wasn't much going on there then, unless a show came to town, and we could see the parade. We loved to see the parade. Sometimes we'd be fortunate enough to catch a ride, and if we didn't, it'd be walk.

It was all dirt roads and homemade bridges made out of thick planks. Them old hills would be hard to climb; it wasn't nothing like it is now. There was no cars.

How often did you go to town for food?

Once a month. We were living on a farm and we raised our chickens, our eggs, our greens, our beans, our meat. Everything except coffee and sugar and flour. We'd get nutmeg in little balls and scrape off whatever we were going to use. We'd put black pepper in a rag and take a hammer and beat it until we got enough to season with.

We'd plant sorghum and ribbon cane, and we had our own syrup mill. Everybody would come. We'd make syrup for everybody in the community. We fattened our hogs on that syrup. In the summer the sorghum would go to sugar, and we didn't have to buy much sugar. There wasn't no granulated sugar like it is now. We'd take fifty cents and buy green coffee. Well, my goodness, you could get four of them tall bags for

fifty cents. Then we'd put it in the oven and parch it just like you would peanuts. When it got brown enough to look like coffee, Mama would break an egg and rub it over that coffee and we'd keep stirring until that egg dried and then she'd lay it out on some paper.

Everybody had coffee mills, and you'd put the coffee in there and grind it up and make your coffee.

We had mills where you could grind your corn when it got too hard to cook. Otherwise, everybody had a grater so they could grate their corn and bring it to the house. And everybody had wood stoves and a big piece of sheet. They'd grate the corn, add milk, make up a whole keg of corn bread, rake back the ashes and put the corn bread down there wrapped up in that wet sheet, put ashes on it, and make the best tasting bread you ever ate. Good and sweet.

When we got ready to cook a cake, we had a Dutch oven that had legs to sit up on. You'd put the cake in this oven, put coals under the bottom of it, put the lid on, put some coals on top, and brown it just like in that oven in yonder. We cooked in things like that.

What did you celebrate?

We'd celebrate the 19th of June and the 4th of July. We'd hurry to get our work done by the 19th of June, and we'd have a big picnic somewhere. Then we were through until the 4th of July. Then there was nothing until Christmas. About a week before Christmas everybody would start to have a month dance. We danced at this place this night and we'd take it from house to house from a week before Christmas until after New Year's. All we danced was the square dance. They had guitars and some had fiddles, some Jews harps, and that was the biggest music we had. We'd go to a dance somewhere every night. Old folks and young folks and all, they'd go in and sit down and enjoy themselves.

How did your family celebrate Christmas day?

We ate dinner at home, and the rest of the day we'd spend going from house to house celebrating. In the summer there was plenty of grapes, and the old people would make us gather them muscadines to make wine. When the fall came, they'd make us pick persimmons and we'd make a big churn of persimmon beer.

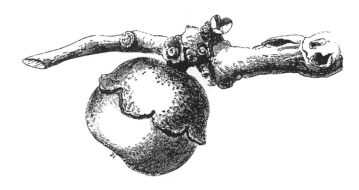

Everybody would cook a cake or two, and somebody would cure a beef, sometimes this one, and then next time somebody else would do it. We'd go from house to house and celebrate, drink the beer and drink the wine they made out of grapes, and it was good. I thought it was.

Did you hang up your stocking by the fire?

Oh yes, hoping that Santa Claus would come see us. We'd have a celebration at church. It was a big church and people would come from everywhere. Children would give little speeches and songs. We thought we were living it up, which we were in them days.

What was your favorite Christmas present?

There was a white family and we lived on their farm until we moved here. Me and my daddy worked there. He'd go and make a fire in the morning so they could get up, and I'd milk the cows until school time. They furnished me with all my school clothes. At Christmas they'd bring us things that we needed, clothes, shoes, hats and things. I never did ask Mama or Daddy for nothing. One Christmas, I was eight or nine years old, and they gave me a gold ring. I got that ring in there yonder somewhere, and a pair

of earscrews and a little matchbox holder. That matchbox holder is hanging up in the kitchen there now.

They had a daughter, Lillian Shackleford, and Miss Lillian was a genius. She went to school for cooking, and all through the day she'd be cooking. I'd hang around up there because I know if they'd eat, I was gonna eat too. She was trying to learn me how to make a chocolate pie. Well, I was a child. There were some chickens in the yards, big old domineckers, and instead of

Fannie's mother.

watching her, I was looking out the window at them chickens. She hauled off and slapped me so hard. I got mad. I didn't say a word, I just walked on out and went on down the hill home.

When I got there, Mama was sitting in the hall sewing on a quilt, and as I got nearer to the house I just went to howling. Mama says, "What's the matter with you?" I told her Miss Lillian hit me. "Why did she hit you?" Well, I told a tale as usual.

She stuck her needle in the quilt and said, "Let's go back up there." I'd rather have a whipping than go back up there. When we got there Mama asked what was the trouble and Miss Lillian just up and told her.

Mama carried a switch with her. She handed the switch to Miss Lillian and said, "If you can't whip her you let me." Miss Lillian said she'd given me enough this time. I went home and Mama gave me a good whipping.

What she was trying to show me, I learned, but I learned it afterwards. I couldn't see that she was learning me to make my living as long as I lived. After I got grown and got married, she called on the telephone and wanted me to come and cook. I went back and went to work, making them cakes and pies and things, just like that child learned me. I liked it all right, but I couldn't see no money behind it then.

I worked there until 1923 and they called me to a big oil field in Hahnville, Louisiana. They called me to cook. I stayed four years cooking for 87 men, then I come home and put all that down and went to farming. I farmed until I was 73 and the doctor told me I'd better put that plow down. I hated to give it up because I like to farm better than anything I've ever done. Shoot, there ain't any place around here that you can look at that I ain't plowed. But I had to give it up.

Did you drive a tractor?

No, that was one thing I never did learn to do. I got scared one morning when I was a kid. There was a mill that handled gasoline and stuff like they got now. I was sitting with my brother, and that mill blew up and killed two men there, and some of the tin blew right over the top of our house. It scared me with nobody at home. I just can't stand no kind of engine. I had a car and a pickup too but I had to be shed of both of them because I couldn't drive. But a pair of mules and a wagon, I could put that anywhere a man could put it.

I plowed all over. I cleared new ground. I've done all kinds of work in the fields. Splitting rails, fixing fence, clearing new ground, cutting wood with a crosscut saw. I ain't seen a knot that I couldn't split. I can split them now if you want me to.

101

Were you ever sick as a child?

Me, sick? I only know being sick once or twice, something like smallpox or measles. Outside of that, we never was sick. We used to eat so much trash I reckon we kept our ownselves cleaned out. I remember papa taking me to a doctor one time. I had been at school and the teacher slapped me so hard she like to give me lockjaw. Mama had to keep a spoon in my mouth all night that night. The next morning my daddy got a buggy and a horse from Mr. Shackleford and he carried me to the doctor. The doctor told papa to give me a tablespoon of Epson salts and some water and the swelling went down. That's the only time I know being at the doctor until I was married. In them days some old lady'd come doctor on you, and that'd be it.

Did you have any home remedies?

Oh yes, that's all we used. People wasn't sickly like they are now. We had a remedy for earache, a big old bug called a blister bug. He's got one drop of blood in him. Whenever we had a ear-ache, Mama would get a blister bug, pull him in two, drop that drop of blood in our ear and put some cotton in there, and it cured it. For toothache, a woman could cure it in a man, and a man could cure it in a woman. The last time I had a toothache was in 1921, and I never have had a toothache no more. The man who cured it said not to tell how. If you tell anybody, it won't do no good.

For ringworm, we'd take one of them fig leaves—they got milk in them—and you drop the milk on the ringworm. When we had a headache we took peach tree leaves or sassafras leaves, beat them up until they were gummy and white, bind our head up with it and that'd cure that headache.

When we had a fever, there is a little weed they call dogfennel. Some call them bitterweed. They'd get that and make us a tea and give it to us. If you had a stomach ache you'd break yourself off a piece of calamus root and chew it a few minutes and it was gone. For bleeding, they'd get soot out of the back of the fireplace. If that didn't stop it, they'd make us a tea called The Devil's Shoe-string. It will stop bleeding.

For sore throat, you get on the north side of a persimmon tree, chip that outer bark off, get you some of that inner bark, make a cup of tea and gargle your throat with it. That's alum and it'll cure you. A red oak tree, the same way, on the north side. We raised catnip for catnip tea to give to babies for hives and fever. It's good for women folks. Garlic was for high blood pressure.

Did you ever have any unusual experiences?

One morning it come up a little mist, and Mama had a sister that lived better than a half mile from us, and she sent me there. I don't remember what she sent me after but in them days they'd tell you to go in a haste, come in a pace, and don't stay long in a place. They meant for you to move on when they tell you that.

Whatever Mama sent me after, I got, and I come on back. On the way back here comes a rain. When I got to the gate, I saw a man standing there. I wasn't but a child and it scared me.

He said, "Come on, I ain't going to hurt you." He spoke nice and kind, and he was a white man. He had on a pair of pants that had a stripe in them, and his shirt had a stripe in it, but he didn't have a hat. He had to be Mr. Asberry Loomis' daddy, but he was dead at the time. I went after him, around the corner of the fence where there was a big double pine tree. I was stepping in his tracks. You know how kids will step in grown folks tracks.

He walked all around this double tree and when I got there, he moved back out of the way, and said, "Right there, right down there." I looked to see what he was talking about and when I looked up, there wasn't nobody but me.

You talk about putting the running on, I got away from there. I lit out. Mama was coming. She asked me, "What's the matter?" I told her. She said, "Let's go see," and we went back. The place he'd pointed to looked like where a salamander had thrown up a mound. I said, "Right there, Mama." She said, "Uh huh, somebody's give you some money there." I didn't know what she meant or nothing. She said, "Come on, we'll go to the house and I'll tell Mr. Smith." That's what she called my daddy. "And we'll go back and get it."

We went to the house and she said, "Don't you tell nobody nothing about it." I didn't tell nobody nothing, and if she had done the same, I'd have got the money. Mama told Daddy, and they got five or six men to go up there. The moon was shining that night just as pretty as ever I saw it shine in my life. Mama wouldn't let us go, so we decided to tiptoe a piece and watch the men. There was a big hickory tree up there and we went on up there, and we had no more than got there, there come one of the awfulest winds. I ain't never seen nothing like that before. The moon was shining just like day, and there wasn't a cloud in the sky, but them limbs blowed so we had to get out of the way. It blowed limbs down in our back yard.

Two or three mornings after that, it come another shower, and my daddy had to go to the white folks' house. I said, "Papa, let me go with you." We went over the hill and we had to go right by this place where the money was. My daddy picked up two pieces of money, a quarter and a dime. He and those men had dug this safe out of the ground right where that man showed me it were, and cut the top out and got the money. I guess it was all for the good, but I always will say, if Mama hadn't told everybody in the country, I might've got that money.

Do you remember any other scary experiences?

I like to got killed in a tornado in 1921, when I was 23. It made up right over Ore City. Me and another girl were plowing for Mr. Ken Brown. He said, "You all take out." We saw it coming on us, walking like a person, just about that high off the ground, and under it was a red streak of fire. We run and when we got to this gate, that thing stood the gate right straight up and taken it and we ain't seen it from that day. We run to the cotton house and it just picked that cotton house up and didn't leave a block. That cotton house went over us, but it didn't tear it to pieces until it got to More.

Well, we thought the cyclone was gone but it come on back and we ran to the syrup mill. There was cedar trees and red oak trees around the syrup mill and we could hear them trees falling. Directly they'd stand up and and go high 'til they got so far and then they'd come down. A pine tree knocked me fifteen feet when the top of it struck me, but it just scared me mostly. We come on to Mr. Brown's house, and I've never seen nothing like that before. The leaves looked like they'd been through a sausage mill.

He had a big old Poland-China sow that weighed over four hundred pounds

and it blowed the sow up on a tree and scalded the hair off her. There was a little hair under her ears and a little at the tip of her tail. The rest of her was as white as if someone had scraped her. She was stuck up there on that big old tree, looked like she was standing up, just dead as she could be. And chickens was sticking all around.

We went to his house, the floor was there, the stove was sitting on the floor, the bed was in the room, the safe was in the corner, the dishes was in the safe, the plates were turned down on the table and not a wall around that house. Not a wall. I hope I never see nothing like that again.

There was a girl had a nine-month-old baby in her arms. She left the house running and it tore that house all to pieces. A piece of two-by-four had broken off and pinned her to the ground. That baby was sitting up in her arms playing, not a scratch on it, and she was just as dead then as she is now. We went into town, and there was a colored woman who ran out of the house with her baby, and it taken that baby and dropped it in a pine thicket. They hunted 'til 11 o'clock the next day before they found it in the pine thicket playing. The baby wasn't hurt but it killed the mother. It knocked her off the porch and just took the baby and carried it on.

There was a white man digging a well in his place, and he had 19 gallons of ribbon cane syrup in the back of a wagon. He had a boy eight or nine years old, and it loaded that boy up under the house. He struck something. It didn't kill him but he never did get over it. It taken that syrup up over the porch and stacked it down in the well, and taken that wagon bed off that wagon, and nobody's seen it from that day 'til this.

But the thing I never could understand, that morning before I went to work, Mama heard me crying in my sleep and she come to see what my trouble was. My baby boy, Jack, that's what I was crying about. I was dreaming something had come and broke his leg and his arm in two places. Mama woke me up and said, "Go on to work." Before I got back, it had done happened, but it wasn't my boy. It was Mr. Barry Brannon's wife, and just like I saw it. That arm broke in two places, and her leg broke in one. She died that night. I don't want to see another tornado.

Fannie's wall of mementos.

How did they treat black people here?

It was rough here. There wasn't a bathroom for the colored, there wasn't nothing. I got on the bus during World War II, and there was a soldier boy was coming in on a furlough. Every little pig trail they got to, this bus driver would stop and take on more people and the soldier had gotten back as far as he could stand up. The bus stopped all of a sudden and the soldier staggered back and stepped on this white boy's foot. The boy's father got up and he knocked that soldier down. The soldier didn't say nothing and he didn't do nothing. When we got to Jefferson, he got off and made a call to NAACP headquarters. This man came here and they put him in jail in Marshall, but he signed folks up for the NAACP.

You get what you want when you want it. I was coming from Houston one night, got on the wrong train so when they stopped the train, I got out. When the right train got to the first crossing in Longview, it had to blow its horn and when it come around that bend I was standing in the middle of the tracks. I stood right there. I didn't get scared. I stood right in the middle of the track and when the engineer see'd that white handkerchief I had, he put the brakes on that train. He brought me right to Jefferson.

Ruben Munguia

Ruben Munguia's family has been in the Americas for more than four hundred years. Born in Mexico, Munguia came to Texas as a child. His family has long been involved in both politics and publishing. Munguia combined those interests in his printing business in San Antonio where he can write and publish political statements.

Ruben, on right, with his brother.

Ruben Munguia

Where were you born?

I was born in Mexico City in 1919, and reared in this country. My parents came to San Antonio when I was a small boy, in 1926.

Where did your family come from?

The first Munguias came to the new world in 1549. They were originally from the Basque province of Biscay, which is in the northeast corner of Spain. Basques do not consider themselves Spaniards as do the Madrilenos and other people of the Iberian peninsula.

Mexican Revolution

Porfirio Diaz governed Mexico, except for one four year interlude, for thirty-four years. He transformed the constitution into a personal dictatorship. By 1910 nearly half of Mexico belonged to less than three thousand families, while nine and a half million farmers were virtually without land. The hacendados lived in Mexico City or Paris, enjoying revenues from the lands their ancestors had taken from the Indians and leaving them to be managed by hired administrators. The absentee owners and other citizens were unaware that under Diaz the peons were slowly starving. Diaz did not believe in a free press and a free judiciary. In 1909 there was a poor harvest, and many peasants died of hunger. The peons demanded "Tierra y Libertad." The Revolution had begun.

Ruben with his father.

My father, Romulo, Sr., was an orphan. He attended school some three years and went to Mexico City from Guadalajara in 1903. He apprenticed himself to a printer and became a journeyman printer. He was very interested in closer international understanding. His early writings had to do with a proposed Pan-American Union that would extend from Argentina to Alaska. He was one of the early advocates of Pan American and hemispheric unity.

He participated in the revolutionary movements in Mexico originating about 1908, not as a soldier, but as a newspaper publicist and organizer of public information forums. He was an alternate to the Constitutional Congress of Mexico held in Queretaro in 1917. He was sentenced to be shot by counter-revolutionary forces but was saved at the last minute by orders from higher up.

I was at that time five or six years old but I remember going to my father's newspaper plant and going with him to political rallies. My daddy never became an American citizen. His love for Mexico was so real he would not change his citizenship. He left Mexico in 1925 because of political persecution. He arrived here in January, and he missed being captured by a couple of days.

My mother, Carolina, was a school teacher. She was educated in the Methodist college in Puebla. She graduated as a teacher, taught in Vera Cruz, then met and married my father. After Papa's departure for the states, Mama stayed in Mexico because they had a newspaper, a home, and some livestock she had to dispose of. In April, 1926, with her three small sons and one baby daughter, she came to the States from Puebla, south of Mexico City. I remember getting on the train and soldiers getting on and off at various stops.

Mama used to tell a tale about me wandering off and going to one of the cars and playing with some of the old soldiers. They were probably fathers who hadn't seen their own children in years and welcomed a young one who reminded them of better days left behind. Mother became frightened because she thought I was lost or something. After I was returned, she kept me close to her until we reached Laredo.

Did it take days and days?

Probably three or four days. Mama fed us. At the stations they had vendors. They also had guys who would come through the train selling candy and drinks and stuff. "Candy butchers," they were called. I remember the train in the middle of the night and the light beams going down the railroad track, and I imagined seeing two silver streaks. When we crossed the border into the states, we came through Laredo. Papa took a chance and went into Nuevo Laredo for us and hired a jitney taxi to drive us to San Antonio. The road out of Laredo was paved for possibly fifteen or twenty miles, and then the car followed the Missouri-Pacific railroad track across the fields. The road into San Antonio was paved also some thirty-five or forty miles out, but between that point and the other point out of Laredo there was nothing but open fields.

111

Ruben, on right,
with his mother, brothers and sister in 1926.

What was your first memory of San Antonio?

The Battle of Flowers Parade. We arrived the week of the parade and we watched it from the lawns at Santa Rosa Hospital. Daddy worked at the newspaper, *La Prensa*, which was across catty-corner from the hospital. I still love parades.

How about your brothers and sisters?

I had one older brother and five younger brothers and sisters. My father was enthusiastic that those of us who had been born in Mexico become American citizens. He ingrained in me and my brothers the obligation to serve our chosen country. My brother Ralph joined the service four days before Pearl Harbor and remained in the service until his retirement some four or five years ago. He wound up a colonel. My brother Bill was drafted in the first year of the war. He retired a Chief Master Sergeant in the Air Force.

I was in the service from 1942 through 1945. I became chief clerk at the Randolph Field printing control office that did all the printing for all bases from Texas to the Pacific Ocean. As the war progressed, men were needed and we installed more equipment and closed the print shops that were in the various bases and did all the printing for the command at Randolph. My brother Romulo and I served only as long as our obligation, which was the duration of the emergency. We came home after the war and have worked as printers all our lives. My brother, Henry, for whom Mayor Cisneros of San Antonio was named, died as a young boy in 1940. I had two sisters, one, Elvida, the mother of Henry Cisneros and the other, Estela, who died three years ago.

112

When you were a teenager, what did you do to have fun?

We did not have the freedom of money, automobiles and telephones teenagers today have. We did have dances of the same type as the Chrysanthemum Ball and the Black and White Ball which today are still the high note of the social season in San Antonio. All of us were working together to be part of something. We would organize social clubs and have small social events. Most of the clubs would elect a queen, which was the winner of a beauty pageant. All of them participated in the Fifth of May and the Sixteenth of September, Mexican patriotic celebrations.

The economies of many families were such that we all did some work. Most of the boys made their own kites, made their own tops and skateboards. We made our own scooters. We made wooden pistols. Do you know what an inner tube is? In my days, every automobile had a bunch of them to inflate the tires. After a tube was punctured several times and could not be repaired anymore, we would take it apart and make wide rubber bands and take the clothes pins from Mama and make rubber guns. We did a little fishing. We would go to the creeks, the lakes, go hunting. We did not mind hiking ten, fifteen miles to go to a ball game.

During spring training season when there were a couple of major teams here

Diez y Seis

September 16, "Deiz y Seis," is Mexican Independence day and celebrates the "grito" or cry for revolt by Father Miguel Hidalgo y Costilla at Dolores on that date in 1810. Aroused by that call, the Indians armed themselves with clubs, knives and machetes and set off with Father Hidalgo and Captain Ignacio Allende to liberate Mexico.

Cinco de Mayo

"Cinco de Mayo" or May 5, is the second most important date in Mexico's history. On May 5, 1861, General Zaragosa, born in Goliad, Texas, defeated French Forces at the Battle of Puebla, temporarily preventing European intervention in Mexican sovereignty. A subsequent French army captured Puebla and Mexico City, and Maximilian of Austria was made Emperor of Mexico.

we'd go to their camps. We would go from Our Lady of the Lake College across the city to Eagle Field. We never thought it was an imposition. Where the bus yards are now, used to be Indian Field where the San Antonio Indians played their home games. It was a beautiful, large, well equipped ball park and along the right field fence ran San Pedro Creek. Where the creek ran around close to the first base line, trees had grown. They were a hundred feet, two hundred feet in the air, and we kids who could not afford to go to the ball game would climb those trees and watch.

Did you have a lot of girl friends?

I don't think that in my early years girls were persons I particularly cared for. Of course I went to school and they were there. But what you call a girl friend I did not have until I met Martha whom I courted and married.

What was dating like then?

I can speak only for the Mexican or Hispanic sector of our society. Since we did not have the automobile and we did not have the money and the freedom that youngsters have today, much of our social life centered around church affairs, school affairs, family affairs. When a couple declared themselves serious about dating and possibly marriage, they could go to the theater or various places. They

generally had a chaperone with them. This was more true among what we call the humble or lower classes than it was among the middle classes and upward.

How did your family celebrate holidays?

Religious holidays, Thanksgiving, Christmas, Easter, Father's Day, Mother's Day, were all celebrated at Mama's house. Generally there would be a big meal, conversation, all kinds of music. Polkas, danzones, waltzes, Scottish, foxtrot. Scottish is like a polka. The polka is the music that developed around the North Mexico rural farm areas. It was played with guitars, accordions, violins. Urban areas had all the finest and most

sophisticated instruments, pianos, lyres, horns, etc.

What kind of vacations did you have?

We did not have planned vacations. We would take off with the folks on weekends. We would take drinks, basket lunches, playthings and enjoy ourselves in the parks that catered to weekend vacations. Many families would get in their cars and camp out at South Padre Island or some similar beach on the coast. They put up a tent and stayed there for a week. We would travel sometimes to see kin folks in other cities.

How about discrimination? Was the Ku Klux Klan big back then?

Yes, I am sure they were. But I am going to be perfectly honest with you. Our family cannot say that we suffered from any discrimination. This comes from a state of mind, I believe. My father and my mother, being educated and proud people, never attempted to force themselves on anybody. They had no reason to look for trouble.

As boys, knowing very little English because we had just come from Mexico, my brother Ralph and I sold *Liberty, Colliers, Saturday Evening Post* and other magazines. Ralph would take a certain sector of the city. I took the sector downtown around the *San Antonio Light*. Never did any of our customers discrimi-

nate against us. We were treated fairly and friendly.

What about the restaurants?

Some restaurants discriminated. Some theaters also, but more toward the black than to the Mejicano. There was more discrimination among Mejicanos themselves. If you go to Mexico, you will note the various society levels and how they interact. You will find there is more discrimination in Mexico than there is here even though they are of the same national origin. Discrimination really is based on economic differences.

What were your favorite and least favorite subjects in school?

I don't believe I had a least favorite subject because I had a job to do. My job was to study. It was a job that had to be done whether it was PE, or Mechanical Drawing, or shop work. But favorites, yes. History and Social Studies. I was a straight A student but I quit school in my first year of high school.

Did you want to quit school?

Yes. I will tell you why. Not because I did not care to go to school but because of the depression, and the fact that at that time our family had seven kids in school, and Daddy had just begun his own business. What I was pursuing was not printing, but in the afternoons, I'd help him in the print shop. I was able to translate and do those things and learn the business from the ground up with him and the other old timers who worked for him.

All my brothers took printing in school so they could have fitted very well into the family's business. My brother, Ralph, who was ahead of me, got a scholarship so he went to college in Austin. I was already out of school helping my dad so that my brother could graduate and I decided not to go back to school because I was a business man. I am not going to recommend to you that you quit school. It depends on what you want to do.

Has printing changed a lot?

It's a totally new industry from when I started printing. Then, almost everything was hand operated. You had to set type and set the presses. Your preparatory work often took as much time as it did to run the job. Today there's very little hand setting and there are machines that will set up a complete newspaper page in seven minutes.

Have you had to retrain yourself?

I've had to adapt myself. You never stop learning. Unfortunately, our printers coming on board now do not have the background that we had of doing everything by hand. We utilized our space

better and combined types and sizes in a more pleasing manner. Today it is slapped together and photographed. That is bad news because our lay people aren't as interested in having something pleasant to read and look at as the old-timers. I guess you could say that goes for most everything today, art for instance, and music. It's a fast food operation.

Would you consider yourself a "workaholic?"

You have never seen a drunk admit that he is a drunkard, have you? My wife tells me I am a workaholic. I hate to fish and I hate vacations. You have twenty-four hours a day. You are going to sleep how many hours? How long is it going to take you to eat your meals? What are you going to do? Every hour is an opportunity, a challenge. If you are going to school, you will be a better scholar by using all the hours available to study. I am not only a worker, I am a manager and a janitor. I do everything. I own my own business, I can't afford to waste time.

What are your religious beliefs?

I am a strong believer in separation of church and state. I look back on history and I can understand, appreciate and be grateful for the many advances the Catholic Church brought to the

Americas. At the same time I can resent the fact that they came and destroyed civilizations and cultures and peoples. The Church in the first four hundred years of colonialism in the Americas extracted a vast percentage of the wealth of Mexico and sent it back to Spain and Italy. If you have ever been in Mexico you've been in churches and can see that somebody spent a lot of money to build gilded altars and castles that could have been used to buy seed, feed babies or things like that.

Do you have strong ideas and beliefs because your father was a political person?

He was a self-educated man, a newspaper man. He made friends with all people. Among the educated people you find the

Ruben as a young military officer.

political leaders and the political thinkers. He became acquainted with Maury Maverick, Sr., C. Ray Davis, Louis Lipscomb, persons from the Anglo community, from the county government, the city hall, teachers, businessmen, workers. He was a leader of many Mexican organizations that then existed, arts groups, fraternal and labor organizations. The Mejicanos organized many things but as their children became leaders in the community, the children gravitated to the Chamber of Commerce and organizations they thought would make assimilation less difficult. They allowed the old organizations to die. They just got older and there was nobody who cared enough to sustain them.

I am a strong believer in politics because politics is the only avenue by which a man makes himself worth something, the only way he makes the community aware of his ideas, the only way he can help the community. When we came back from the war, we had new financial opportunities, the opportunity for more and better education. It took us five years to get some of the fruits of the new thinking. That's when the Mexican-Americans in San Antonio broke into politics with Henry Gonzalez, Albert Pena, and Albert Trevino as our leaders.

Do you write political statements?

I have. One is the history of the pecan strike in San Antonio. Another has

117

to do with water and what we ought to be doing about conservation. I wrote one that is called, "A Cotton Picker Finds Justice," a review of the Hernandez case and how Gus Garcia, Carlos Cadena and John Herrera went to the Supreme Court and won a major civil liberty case.

Have you ever run for office?

It's more interesting to work like I do. King-makers don't run for office. Political aspirants seek my advice, ask me to prepare their messages, etc. That's what I love. I can put in my own beliefs and hope they are beneficial. And if this candidate should win, I would believe I have served my community.

Thomas Paine and Benjamin Franklin weren't just printers. I'm very proud of our craft. If there had been no Gutenberg in the fifteenth century to make possible the economical means of printing, we'd still be living in a primitive society controlled by monks, kings, and bishops. We wouldn't have books, we wouldn't have telephones or automobiles. We wouldn't have the education and thinking that is now available to all. I regret that printers today are interested in a paycheck primarily, and few appreciate the opportunities they have to teach and to lead.

But you see a printer as a member of the media?

No, not a member of the media. A printer *is* the media.

118

Wanda Ford

Wanda Ford is great-granddaughter of the first postmaster of San Antonio, and daughter of the curator of the Spanish Governor's Palace. Her life, and that of her late husband, architect O'Neil Ford, has been intricately involved with San Antonio. A member of the Conservation Society, she has been a driving force in the attempt to preserve and honor San Antonio's history and historical buildings.

Wanda Ford

Where did your family come from?

My grandmother was born in San Antonio in the place where the building called the Tower Life building stands. Before that it was the Transit building, and before the First World War it was the Smith-Young Tower. My husband, architect O'Neil Ford, always called it "cook stove Gothic" architecture.

Grandmother's father was the first postmaster in San Antonio and I remember grandmother saying that after she was born, her mother sat up in bed and sorted the mail. Post master was a volunteer, not a paid position. It was something that you did for your community. Like so many things in the olden days,

121

Wanda's grandmother

Why did your family settle in San Antonio?

The water. That's how San Antonio became the city that it was, because of the fact that it had the life-giving qualities that a city needs. The people who came here to settle came through the deserts of Mexico, and if you have ever driven to Laredo or Monterrey you know how dry and dusty it is. When they came to this area where there were springs, plenty of fresh water, they knew this was the place to build a community.

The river went right through the downtown area and made a horseshoe bend. Then there was a flood in 1918 or 1922 and the engineers, who did not think much of what we call amenities, the pleasant qualities of life, decided the way to combat flooding was to cut off the bend and to pave right over it. The real estate developers and the city council saw it as a good way to make additional income. That was the beginning of the Conservation Society's influence. There were a few ladies who decided it

people gave of their time to the city because of the joy of being part of its development.

The San Antonio River at Willow Way.

122

Wanda's mother.

jewels of San Antonio were: five ancient missions. The Alamo is the first mission, then Concepcion, San José, Espada, and San Juan, all along the river. Each has its own "acequia."

In this area, in the early days of the Conservation Society, much of the land was being used for gravel pits. Since Mother worked, she took my brother and me on outings whenever she was able. Some early Sunday mornings we would ride south of town and along the way Mother would point out the different

San José Mission.

shouldn't be done because the river was what gave San Antonio its meaning—the beauty and all the things that go along with the natural gifts that a river brings.

How did you get this place?

We lived in Beacon Hill, but Mother, her name was Elizabeth Orynski Graham, decided that the area south of town was being neglected. It was where our real

places and the things of interest and importance to the early days of San Antonio. That is the way that I really learned from the time I was four years old.

In the area of San José Mission one day, we came down a gravel road by some ancient willow trees and stopped because my brother had seen a lot of doves. We made our camp there and

123

Mother spotted a sign that said "For Sale." She took down the telephone number to inquire because she realized that this was part of the old San José Mission orchard and vineyard land.

Mother decided to telephone the number and find out the possibility of buying the land, and she found out the owner, Charles Sutton, was a close friend. I am surprised that Mother even thought about buying the land at that time because her salary was almost nothing at the Spanish Governor's Palace where she was "curator." She did all kinds of things like the janitorial work and cleaning up outside the Palace when they had carnivals, etc. It was about 1930, when the banks were failing.

This is the way I remember it: Mr. Sutton said she wouldn't be able to buy the whole forty-two acres. She thought it was important to keep the area in one piece, but did not have enough money to do that. As I remember it, she paid whenever she could, whatever amount she could. Any little amount she could scrape together. It took a long time.

Because Mr. Sutton gave her such a good deal, Mother decided to give the land for the Mission County Park so that the area would always be open rather than developed as tourist camps or trailer parks. She was grateful to the fates that let affairs work out the way they did for her.

Willow Way as it was.

Tell us about the house.

During the depression, many of San Antonio's old buildings were being torn down, in spite of the efforts of the Conservation Society. Mother decided that at least these bricks and stones and old door frames and windows should be saved, so she would buy them for our house. If you look up there by the big double-hung window over the portico that sticks out, there are some window frames and stone ledges that she got out of the old buildings that were being torn down.

In our association as we were growing up, we had a gentleman who was a carpenter. His name was Juan. We had a wonderful sewing lady named Mrs. Rodriguez, and she had a husband who had fallen and was flat on his back and couldn't move. At that time there was no workman's compensation, and the company for which he worked had no kind of insurance. Mrs. Rodriguez had three children: Josephine, Andrew, and a younger boy named Joe. Andrew was going to have to stop high school and go to work, so Mother said that if Juan, the carpenter, would take Andrew as an apprentice and find a stone mason to work with them, she would pay them a dollar a day to come out and start building her a one-room house here "in the country."

So, with Andrew and Juan and a mason, the stone and other parts of the house were built. But it was very slow because anytime that any of them could get a job elsewhere they were supposed to do that. That was the understanding. They would work for Mother for meager wages and would get other jobs for more money whenever they could.

By the time they started on the one room, we all began to love it here. We were calling this area Willow Way because the way we came was by the willow trees that had been planted in the early days by the Franciscan monks who started Mission San José. Willow trees love the water and also make good

Wanda as a university student.

125

The Spanish Governor's Palace

A man taught Mother to read the doors at the Spanish Governor's Palace from the top down on one, then up on the other. The doors are the same. They have dragons here and shields here and then flowers and fruit down here and there are four central squares. One is a baby, and one is an Indian, and one is the mask of a medicine man, and the conquistadors. From the mother country over the sea (the seashells), through many dangers (the dragons), they came to the infant country of America (baby), bringing their arms for protection (shields). They came to this land of flowers and plenty where they found the Indian. Those are the only two things that are different. On the other door are the conquistadors who came to this land of flowers and with their arms conquered the dangers (dragons again and the mask of the medicine man) and declared the land for the mother country over the sea, and there are the seashells at the top.

holders of the earth, stabilizing the soil. It is also very interesting how plans change as life changes. For instance, Mother, being curator at the Spanish Governor's Palace, decided she liked the stairway there and she incorporated that into her plans for the house. Well, if you have a stairway, you need something to go up to, so that meant she had to build a second story. And when the fireplace was being built, her theory was that as long as you were going to build a chimney you might as well build a fireplace on the other side, and then one upstairs with separate flues, so that's why we have four fireplaces on the first chimney. But it all started with just that one room.

The upstairs had a room for Grandmother and a room for Mother. Then I came from the university and asked Mother where my room was to be. I played the piano and there was no room for that. Poor Mother, trying to build one room to get a place to write a book and it ends up that she has to make a place for the piano. So a long room was added and on the other side of that she built what is the library with all kinds of books, and that is where she was going to do her writing. So that meant a fireplace in that long room where the family portraits are located, a fireplace for Mother, and on the other side another fireplace and a fireplace upstairs for my brother's room since by this time he had come home from college and asked where his room was.

What advantages or disadvantages do you have living in this house?

I never seem to have enough time to get everything in its place. When a lot of things were done, we did not have an architect. Mother just took a stick and drew the plans on the ground. I remember when O'Neil came to San Antonio to do La Villita's restoration. Mother was one of the Conservation Society people worried about what this "Yankee from Dallas" was going to do to La Villita. Mother said that they would invite O'Neil to Willow Way and ask him to bring his plans for La Villita. He charmed those ladies. Everything he said made sense. He came to Mother and said that the house was exquisite, and asked how did she built it so. She was a bit sassy and said "because I did not have an architect." He said, "You are absolutely right, because an architect will sometimes overwhelm a client."

What you would like for Willow Way to be in fifty years?

I hope it is much like it is now, if that is possible, but I don't think anything can stay the way it is. I would like for it to be a place for people to enjoy the kinds of things that are worth enjoying, the natural beauty, the pecan trees, understanding nature, and being a part of the inheritance of the area, the missions and what they stood for, the people who came teaching religious thought. I would like it to be a place for people.

Wanda and her brother in costumes for a festival.

Would you like it turned into a natural preserve?

I thought of that. I think keeping some of the natural creative talents in the area would be very important. Because of machines and technology we are losing the human touch to some of our life, like weaving and pottery making, wood carving and stone work.

I would rather have the house used. It would be interesting if we could have a place where people could come and carve and paint and do whatever they can do, but I am worried about the elite quality of places like that. They appear not to be part of the world. On the other hand we need a kind of seclusion to be creative.

When you think of the kinds of things you want to do in your city, what do you think is most important?

Dreaming about it. When you dream, you plan to do something about it. What kind of dreams do you have? Soon you are going to have to contribute your talents to your community. You are going to have to take over these things that everybody else is doing now.

Do the things that you feel are important to your life and your home and your family, I think those are the first things that you think about. You are born with a place, the meaning of the place you grew up in. If you are a close

family then it is more meaningful. If you are not, you can be close in the sense of the community itself. You can be part of that and contribute to it.

We all have different things to give. We have different ways of living and different kinds of things are important to us. I don't like to kill anything, and I don't like to throw things away, always thinking I can use old things for something else.

We should all make whatever place we are in as good as can be. That's what a sense of history makes you feel, a sense of what makes life important, what makes it a beautiful, challenging, inspirational, delightful place to be. One of the neatest things in the world is free, if you get up as I do and see the sun rise, watch the clouds, hear the birds and smell the flowers.

Eck and Leroy Horton

Eck and Leroy Horton were born on the Horton Ranch, where they have spent their lives except for military service during World War II. Their abiding interest is preserving a way of life that combines hard work with a knowledge of soil, weather, crops, grasses, and domestic and wild animals.

Leroy, left, and Eck, right.

Leroy and Eck

Eck and Leroy Horton

Where were you born and when?

Leroy: On this ranch, about two miles up the road, in 1920, February 29, leap year.

Eck: I was born December 2, 1918, in the same place, a one room camp house in the corner of this field. It had a lean-to kitchen on it. I have lived here all my life, except each of us spent four years in the service. Our parents were Lou and Mary Horton. Lou Horton was

Photo by Dan Klepper

born in San Antonio in 1880. Mother was born in the mountains in 1888. This canyon is called Little Blanco Canyon. Over the mountains there is Big Blanco Canyon and that's where she was born.

This ranch and the ranch east of here used to be all one ranch, something like eight

Mary Horton.

thousand acres. These two old men had it and they built a house over on the Sabinal river. It was a three or four room house on the river, and one of them picked up his two rooms and brought them over here on a wagon when they split this ranch. All that old rough lumber in there was hauled out from San Antonio on an ox cart. Them old boards are still in

the inside walls. My folks moved into the house in 1908. That spring was the only water on the whole ranch.

Have you been a rancher all your life?

Leroy: We've always made our living by ranching and farming. Eck does most of the ranching. We do quite a bit of farming now and I'm the tractor man, he's the horse man. I kind of backed into farming as a hobby at first, and then I got into it full time. We put in our full time as cowboys until I went into the service. The most mechanical thing we had was an old gasoline pump engine. Everything else was horse and wagon. You grow up with it and it comes natu-

The Hortons' birthplace.

ral. We learned to ranch by doing.

Eck: Very little of it was voluntary. It was required of us to do our part each day. We didn't get an allowance, we got our clothes and our shoes, something to eat and a place to sleep.

Leroy: We had our own chores to do and one of us would do one thing and one another. We got up about 6:30. We didn't pay much attention to time then. We had a wood stove and somebody had to bring in wood every night, summer and winter, and we had three different sizes, kindling to start the fire, cedar for a quick fire, and oak. We had three boxes that had to be filled. Winters were pretty miserable. We didn't have nice warm houses or fancy clothes to keep

warm. We had a wood stove in the kitchen and one in the living room.

We raised turkeys. As soon as we got big enough we trapped for furs in the winter. That was how we got part of our money. We sold pole cats and possums and stuff like that.

Eck: We had a lot of chickens to feed and gather the eggs. We had a hog or two to feed and we milked a bunch of cows and sold butter. The cows had to be tended to every night. Every morning we got on a horse and rode somewhere. Then we had screw worms which you all probably don't know anything about. In the summer time it was continuous. You had to check on livestock every day and doctor them. They've eradicated those now. We don't see our stock probably once a week and then in a pickup.

Does it get lonely out here?

Eck: Never.

How did you water?

Leroy: We used to have one gasoline pump that watered the whole place

Working with the cattle.

133

Leroy and Eck in front of a backyard tent.

from the spring. We didn't have any pipe line or wells. We had to dig about 500 feet for water. We had an Eclipse windmill with wooden blades. I guess it was pretty to look at but it wasn't much for pumping water. We didn't have any water back in the mountains; the stock had to walk out to get a drink. That was all one big pasture. We have plenty of drinking water for the stock now but for crops we have to wait until it rains. If we don't have rains for the grass we have to feed the cattle out of the barn or buy feed.

What did you do in your spare time when you weren't working?

Leroy: We rode over to the river nearly every day looking at stock and in the summer time we always took a swim. There wasn't bathing suits in those days. We didn't play games at home because there was just the two of us. We didn't take vacations. We didn't work all the time but there was always something to do and people didn't go places like they do now.

Eck: In our teen years we went to San Antonio and visited our cousins. If we went to San Antonio that was considered our year's vacation.

134

A highlight was Saturday afternoon. Everybody went to town Saturday afternoon. They got there about two o'clock and stayed 'til five and that was the weekend. They parked the cars on the streets and the mamas got in the car with somebody else and visited and the men sat in the barber shop or sat on the corner and visited and the kids usually went to the picture show. I can count up the times I went to movies on my fingers.

On Sunday afternoons we'd get with some of the neighbors and go over to the river and go swimming or go out and rope my daddy's calves. If somebody was real liberal they'd buy a fifty pound block of ice and come out to the ranch and make ice cream.

What is your brand?

Eck: It's a square and compass. Some people call it the Double X. It's been in our family for over a hundred years.

Did you have a close relationship with your parents?

Leroy: I would say we did. We respected them and loved them. We never give it any thought but that's the way it was.

Eck: We always believed in whatever our folks said. We took it for what they meant and done it and went on about our business. When one family stays

together that long I guess that they believe in hard work.

Did you get your mouth washed out with soap?

Leroy: A switch took care of all that. Our folks never did have petty deals like that. If you deserved something you got the switch and that was the end of it.

What did you want to be when you grew up?

Eck: I wanted to be a rancher. I never thought of being anything else.

Leroy: When I was five or six years old I wanted to be a banker and have a two-story house. I was going to let Mama live upstairs. Bankers were big shots in a town like Sabinal and everybody had to go to the banker for whatever they needed. I guess I almost made it. I built a two story house and I've been a director on a savings and loan. I don't think a banker has near the respect I thought he had.

I also admired Red Hill, who was a cowboy that floated around the country. All the youngsters liked him because he had a lot of tall tales to tell. Any time he'd ride up to somebody's house they'd unsaddle his horse and turn it loose in the trap and he'd stay there until he found something better. He could spend hours and days talking about his experiences. A lot of Mexican families went to town in wagons on Saturday to do their shopping. Red could speak Spanish and he'd stop and visit with them and we'd have to drive the cattle on, and he'd catch up, and about that time another wagon would come along and he'd spend another hour back visiting.

He got married when he was up in his fifties and that's the nearest thing he ever had to having a home. He never worried about anything. I guess you'd call him a bum now, but he was anything but that. I guess he had one of the most enjoyable lives of anybody that ever was.

How did you celebrate Christmas?

Leroy: Christmas would always be a big deal. We had a Christmas tree and got a few presents. We didn't get presents every occasion that came along so we really appreciated Christmas.

Eck: On Christmas Eve we cut a cedar tree and put it up in the house. Daddy would take us out in the pasture and we stayed until about dark. When we came back the tree was decorated with presents under it. While we were in the pasture, Santa Claus was supposed to have come and left

the presents. The first trees I can remember had candles that was strapped on the limbs. We come in and ate supper and had our Christmas. We maybe had some kinfolks out for Christmas day but that was about it.

Leroy: They had a rope they put around the tree, and tinsel and a few

Leroy as a teenager.

hanging ornaments of some kind. Mama always baked animal cookies with hard sugar icing, and she hung those on the tree and then she'd hang apples by the core. They all disappeared in a day or two.

Eck: One of the greatest treats was to eat an orange and an apple. That was the only time we ever had them.

What was social life like?

Leroy: After we were teenagers there were Saturday night dances in the homes. Somebody cleaned out their living room and bedroom and invited everybody over for what they called house parties. One home would have it one Saturday night and another one the next. The older people would play Forty-two and the younger kids got out in the yard and played whatever games they played.

Eck: The kids just ran and screamed. We played a lot of hide-and-go-seek. That was our big game in the dark. There wasn't no lights then. It wasn't boring. We went to the dances with our parents. Parents were the ones that instigated it and the children were glad to go along.

Leroy: We never did have a dance here. We got in line one time and cleaned the front two rooms out and rolled up the rug and it rained and nobody ever got there.

Eck: After a few years the city boys got to horning in and that broke it up. They'd hang around on the outside and pick up some of the girls and that led from one thing to another and that broke it up.

Leroy: I never had a bona fide date until I was about eighteen years old. That was about standard then. I dated a neighbor girl on Saturday night. It was just a once a week deal then. We'd go to a dance somewhere, go to a picture show. We always double or triple dated. You didn't go off by yourself. We'd end up at a cafe and get a bite to eat. We was always home by twelve o'clock.

Where did you go to school?

Leroy: Trio School, a two room brick building. We went two years in Sabinal to high school. Trio High School closed the year we went to Sabinal in 1934.

Eck: It was a country school five miles down the road. We went from nine to four. Most of the time we rode horses to school. We'd leave early in the morning and ride there and leave our horse and come home after school. There were three different rooms for eleven grades. The first, second and third in one room, fourth, fifth, sixth in another room, and then seventh, eighth, ninth, tenth, and eleventh was upstairs.

Leroy: My ambition was to get upstairs where I could see. The year I qualified, they turned the classes around and put the little kids upstairs so I never did make it up there.

Eck: At one time there was a hundred and thirty from the first grade through the eleventh. I imagine there were fifteen to eighteen children in a class most of the time. It varied.

Leroy: That was during the height of the depression. A lot of folks had moved in with relatives, any place where they could squat. Some of them lived in tents, but there was houses all over that prairie down there. Most of the farms had at least three houses on them and nearly all of them had somebody living in them.

Eck: Everybody at school took their lunches. There were some kids that didn't have enough for lunch.

Leroy: We took sandwiches. A frijole bean sandwich mashed with mustard on it. A scrambled egg sandwich with bacon or sausage. Then we had some kind of sandwich with preserves on it. We had a good lunch. We didn't have no baker bread. Mother baked bread twice a week. The most important thing was something to wrap your lunch in. Some neighbor was eating high on the hog and we got the bread wrappers to wrap our sandwiches in and we brought them back home. We recycled brown paper bags and our wrappings. Otherwise lunch was wrapped in newspaper. Mama made us a canvas satchel that we put our lunch in and hung on the saddle, and another that we put our books in.

Did the Depression have any effect on you?

Leroy: I was very aware of the depression, still am. My daddy never owned much property before the depression. He had a little working capital and the banks kept after him to borrow some money, and he and his partner leased a place and bought a bunch of cattle. They didn't own them six months until they weren't worth anything. They bought them for eighty dollars a head and kept

The Hortons' father, Lou Horton.

them for three years and sent them to Kansas and got thirty dollars a head for them.

He took in a goat and sheep partner. They fenced these mountains and bought a bunch of goats and went deeply into debt and in a year's time all he had was paper. They give eight dollars a head for the goats and I guess mohair was bringing seventy or eighty cents a pound when they bought them. They sheared them three times and the first two shearings they couldn't sell and had to put in a warehouse and when they finally sold it they got a nickel a pound which barely paid for the shearing.

But he never did quit. He never got even until not too long before he died. He used to go to Mama for a quarter when we went to town. He never carried a billfold, never carried any money in his pocket. He didn't have any use for it I guess.

Eck: The only money we had we got from chickens, milk cows, turkeys. We sold eggs and butter to buy necessities. All the money that Daddy made went to the bank for a period of seven or eight years. I know he walked the floor at night for years trying to figure out what to do. That went on all our teenage years. We didn't do without anything, we didn't suffer, we just didn't have anything extra.

Leroy: After we went to school in Sabinal we got twenty-five cents a week for spending money. We rationed it out a nickel a day and bought a sody pop or some candy. You could get a milk shake for a nickel. It had a little milk in it but was mostly water. That was a big decision to have to make. My favorite was Delaware Punch. It come in a three sided bottle. We had plenty to eat but we never had money for any kind of luxury.

Eck: We were fortunate that we had a place we called home. Nearly all this land between here and Sabinal changed hands during the depression. People just walked off from it or lost it. They moved around from one little place to another.

What did you like best about school?

Leroy: Recess. We played baseball and whatever was in season. Tops, marbles. The girls played jacks and hopscotch. I guess my least favorite thing was English.

It was easy to get in trouble in school. Spanking was part of their reward for teaching I guess. One of our teachers was absent one day and there wasn't no such thing as a substitute teacher. They went upstairs and got one of the high school girls to conduct classes that day and she lost control early in the morning. It turned into a real shootout with spitball shooting and eraser throwing.

Eck: We had four grades in one room, probably twenty-five or thirty kids. They all tried to see what they could get away with that day, acting silly and the boys going to sit with the girls or something else. The next day the first thing, the girl had to go and tell the teacher so and so did this and John did this. The superintendent called us all up there. I think there was twenty-two of us lined up, every boy in that whole room.

Leroy: Of course the superintendent was upstairs all the time that was going on but he didn't stop it. They lined us up according to size and started on the big ones first. I was one of the littlest ones and I was pretty scared by the time he got to me. He give me a good thrashing even though I was at the end of the line. He hadn't got tired.

Eck: He had an off strap, a big leather strap you put on your saddle girth, that's what they used for a whipping strap. Some of them boys went home with blood in the seat of their pants. That was just normal. The teachers weren't restrained from thrashing you. There were no favors from any teachers. If you did anything real good they'd give you a little gold star by your name.

What kind of clothes did you wear to school?

Leroy: Not very many bought ones. Mother made our shirts and underwear out of feed sacks or salt sacks. I don't guess she made our trousers but she made our knee pants. I think we were out of school before we ever got a store-bought haircut.

Leroy: We didn't wear shoes except when it was cold. They kind of got in your way. I was a senior in high school when I got my first pair of boots. Kids didn't wear blue jeans to school in Sabinal. We wore dress pants that was pressed. When I was a senior, it come a rain and I had to ride horseback to take my final exams. I put my boots and blue jeans on. It was looked down on then.

Eck: We wore straw hats.

Leroy: Dad had a partner that I always thought dressed top of the line. Mr. L. O. Carter. He was a small man to begin with and he wore a hat about twice as big as anyone else ever wore. I never knew him even in his old age to wear anything but boots. I don't guess he ever had a pair of shoes. The first big hat I ever got was one of his discarded ones. I had to cut about two inches off the brim to where I could see out from under it.

Did you have the usual childhood illnesses?

Eck: I think chicken pox was all we ever had. I got the measles as soon as I got in the service. I never got the mumps until one of our kids brought it home from school. People used to have the flu in the wintertime. That was a dread. It must have been pretty serious. We took a round of laxative every so often. If you said a cross word to your Mama she'd give it to you. If you got a little cross or a little grouchy, you needed it. You'd stick your tongue out and if it was pale, they'd give you a laxative.

Leroy: I had a lot of earaches until I had my tonsils out. Daddy would get up and light a cigarette and blow smoke in my ear. Mama would warm oil in a

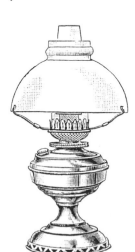

spoon over the kerosene light and pour that in my ear. They made a little horehound candy for coughs. It was pretty vile. When we could eat it we ate a lot of it but when you had to take it for medicine it was nasty.

Eck: We had our tonsils out when we were ten or eleven

years old. They had a special day and signed up seven or eight kids. That was the fad then to get your tonsils out. The doctor's office was upstairs in a two story building on Main Street. You had to climb outside stairs to get there and I always said if you could get upstairs he could save you. All the windows was open and he'd stick that stick in your mouth and look down your throat and when he got through the cotton swabs went out the window.

They had a kitchen table set up in the room and some oil cloth on it. They'd lay you on that table and put an ether mask over your face and tell you to take a deep breath. The last thing I heard them say was, "I think this one's ready." They had three beds set up in the waiting room and they carried you back there until you come to and quit bleeding. They give you an hour or two and then away you'd go. There was a drugstore downstairs in that building and the big deal was they let you have a little dab of ice cream that afternoon. That night the doctor took Mama and Leroy and me up to his house and put us to bed where he could watch us if anything happened. The rest of the kids were from town. The next day we come back here. I never did have any particular trouble with my tonsils but the year after I had mine out I grew more than I had in the three years prior to then. I guess it helped.

Where did you go to town?

Leroy: Sabinal. Sabinal hasn't changed that much. The population is a little larger now than what it was, but quite a few of the businesses are closed. People go to the bigger towns to do their shopping.

Eck: I was happy with the way it was. They had everything we needed, and now they don't have building materials and hardware. You have to go thirty-five or forty miles to a doctor any way you go at it. The nearest hospital is Uvalde or Hondo. If you can make it to the hospital you've got a chance of living.

What is your opinion about how things have changed?

Eck: I never was interested that things should stay the same. I believe the ranch looks better today than it used to. This used to be solid brush. We cleared that out. The cedar used to be up in the mountains and now it's down here. There used to be lots of live oaks but during the fifties when we had a drought they died. We don't ride all day any more, but very seldom a day goes by that I don't ride a horse a little bit. You still can't operate without horses. You have to have them back in the mountains.

Leroy: That tree down there by the fence is well over two hundred years old. It hasn't changed any. I've known it sixty years.

Eck: It seems like we had more cold weather when we were younger. I remember going to school I froze to death trying to get there and back. I don't know how cold it was, since we didn't have a thermometer on the place, but there was ice on the creeks two or three inches thick.

Leroy: There's been a lot of changes in gadgets. My mama had a flashlight when we were young but you only used it on special occasions. A flashlight and batteries were very scarce. We had kerosene lanterns. If we had to go out to the barn we'd take the lantern. You could see about three feet with one of them.

Eck: I guess the biggest difference in a household is refrigeration. We never had ice in the house until I was grown. We had a milk window built on the north side of the house. It was a three by four foot pan with two inches of water in it and a wire frame over it and a cloth over that. The water soaked up that cloth and evaporated. You laid your butter and milk under it and it air-cooled it. After twenty-four hours you could throw it out to the chickens or hogs. You had to replace things each day.

Leroy: We got a kerosene refrigerator when we were sixteen or seventeen. We thought we were real uppity. They were around $350 then which was a year's wages. Anybody that worked for wages got a dollar a day from sunup to sundown. That refrigerator was quite a luxury.

Eck: Folks have got an easier life, and that's part of the problem. It's the idle time and putting in a day trying to make yourself useful. I can remember when we rode wagons and mules pulling them and when we went into what was called "Model T days." My daddy got his first car in 1924, I believe it was. I was married; it was 1946 before I got a car. Couldn't afford one.

What would you like to pass on to your children and grandchildren?

Eck: We'd like to pass this land along but it's getting very difficult.

Eck, Leroy and friends with the new car.

They've got this land valued so high the inheritance tax is prohibitive. Our goal for thirty years has been to fix it so we could pass the ranch on, but with the tax laws it's awful hard.

Leroy: I've got two neighbors that have been bought out and it's already made a difference. We've got coyotes and wild hogs that we didn't have before. The buyers are only interested in recreation or entertainment.

Eck: My boy in Conroe was here the other day and he can't get out in the country down there. He don't have a place like this to go to.

Leroy: After you get older you feel sorry for what your parents went through trying to do without and worrying and providing. You feel like maybe they got short changed. We had about all we could have wanted.

John Banks

The late John Banks grew up on a farm near Seguin. He did not achieve his childhood dream of being a mortician, but he did become the first recognized black Folk Artist in Texas. With his art, Banks recreated the memories and magic of his childhood.

John Banks

You were brought up on a farm?

Yes. My grandfather raised me. He took me when I was around nine years old, after my parents separated. At that time he had seven children of his own at home and I was the eighth. Then later on, he had two more grandchildren. So, we all had a chore to do. We had to work just to have clothes to wear. We worked year around, including Sundays.

What were your chores?

Taking care of the horses, cows and things. I learned how to harness a horse to a plow when I was ten or twelve years old. When I went to school, we had morning chores before going to school and in the evenings after we came home. My main chore around the house was cutting wood. Each of us had one special thing that he did in the morning when he first woke up. I had to get in the stove wood. When I got smart enough, I'd get in my stove wood at night so I didn't have to go out there early in the morning, because I was afraid of rattlesnakes and there were plenty of them around.

Then I would go out and put hay in the stalls for the cows. My grandmother and my older auntie had to milk. That's when you had to sit down and actually milk. They milked three cows every morning, and I had to feed them. If you feed the cows while milking, they'll give more milk and more cream. After I did that, breakfast would be on the table and I would eat. When school was out, we had field work to do. There was always something to do on a farm. We didn't have time to play around, never. When it was wet, my grandfather would send us down in the pasture to cut fence posts and cut wood. We had to do that all day. You worked for your living. We didn't come home for dinner. They would send our dinner out to the field or pasture where we were, and we would take a break, thirty or forty minutes, and go back to work. Then we'd leave in time to come home and feed all the stock before supper. This was every day.

It was so different from your life now. They didn't go to the market like you do now and pick out your meat and your steaks. They had to cut all these things themselves. See this little girl, here. She's churning with one of the old type churners. They would churn cream until it turned to butter. We ground our own coffee. Coffee came just like beans. We waited 'til it dried and then we would parch it. We'd grind it and we had coffee. We had to prepare wood every

Back then we had silent movies. You had to read some to enjoy the movie. There was no sound to it. They cut the picture off and you'd read, but you had to read awfully fast. Then they'd snap the reading off and you'd have the picture come back on. I remember when I heard my first sound picture. It wasn't talking. You only heard the singing part and the rest of it was silent.

I can remember the first radio I ever heard. My dad bought my mother a Victrola which you had to wind to play. He put this record on and they started singing and making music and it was a strange thing for us. It was a miracle.

night and every morning so they could cook. We didn't have gas. The mother's over here making the bread. This was the black people. The other people, the whites, did the same. Maybe they were a little better equipped.

My grandfather would work us all week, and then every Saturday, if he had it to spare, he would give each one of us fifty cents when we got ready to go to town. This Saturday he might pay some, and next Saturday he'd keep them home and let someone else go, because he didn't have fifty cents to give everybody.

What would you do in town?

What did a kid want in town? Candy, soda water. Walk around and look at the people on the street. Go to the movies.

What was your grandfather like?

I think he was a great man. I don't know of anyone who disliked him. My grandfather was a man who couldn't read his name, but what I loved about him was his word. Put your mind and heart to it, so that when you have children one day, your children will have confidence in what you say. You may be ever so poor but a man or a woman with a word will be rich, and people can trust in you, and when you speak people will

149

listen to you. But when you live your life carelessly, and I might say, raggedy, people won't believe you.

I've seen my grandfather cry because he promised a man that he would pay him at a certain time and he didn't have the money and he'd say, "Well, I got to stick to my word," and he'd go and sell the milk cows. The man he sold the cows to, within a month, called my grandfather to come get his cows. "Ben, you come up here and get your cows. I know you need them. You can pay me when you finish the crop." A farmer works all year 'til he harvests the crop and that is the only time he has money, unless he's got an extra job.

Was it poverty?

It really wasn't poverty, because you had your chickens, you had the eggs, you had the cows, and mostly you had corn bread more than flour. You had to buy flour. In the country you had to buy flour, coffee, sugar. My grandmother had a plum orchard and a peach orchard and planted two acres of a garden. She made preserves. She used to put up watermelon rind preserves, peach preserves, tomato preserves, and when she ran out of caps she would take beeswax and pour it over the preserves. It would serve as a top. Very seldom did she sell the preserves; she gave them away.

John's grandmother, Ada McIntire

When my grandfather killed a hog, he'd make sausage and take the fat part of the hog and cook it until it turned to lard. He would pour it in five-gallon cans and when he made sausage he put it down in the cans of lard and if you went out and took the sausage out six months later, it would be just as fresh as the day you put it in. We seldom got a chance to buy ice. By the time you rode a horse there and bought fifty pounds of ice, when you got back home, there wouldn't be much left.

We used to bake bread. We called it light bread, and we had to slice it. Grandma used to make tea cakes and gingerbread. She would bury wood and burn it, and take the ashes and sift it out, and put the ashes in water until it boiled, and then put in corn. When the corn was done, she washed it two or three times and the corn was white as paper. This was hominy, and we ate a lot of hominy in those days. People made soap with ashes which was real white. Lye soap turned yellow, but ash would turn it white.

Swimming in the tank

Money was slow but we raised everything we ate. We never got hungry. People did not have to pay utilities. We used kerosene for lamps. It was about five cents a gallon. Gasoline wasn't over ten cents a gallon.

What was your house like?

It was a house that never had been painted. The yard was filled with chickens and turkeys that my grandmother had. We walked down the road to school every day. I think the school was about a mile and a half from my house.

Tell us about the windmill.

We used the windmill to pump water into a cistern, and this was water for the house and the cattle. The horses stayed at the bottom of the pasture where there was Elm Creek. We used to go back there to the creek and drink the water. Grandfather had a house a little larger than this one that he stored corn in and different stuff. And there was what you call a tank. We used to go swimming there. There was an oak tree about eighty to a hundred feet high.

We jumped from the tree into the tank and swam. We didn't swim in the creek because it had too many water moccasins. We fished there.

The house is not there any more. Nothing is there except the windmill. The whole thing is a pasture now. All of this has grown back into pasture. Most of it is memory.

Juneteenth

John's drawing of "Juneteenth"

Approximately two months after the surrender of General Robert E. Lee at Appomattox that ended the Civil War, Major Gordon Granger landed at Galveston on June 19, 1865, and declared freedom for the slaves in Texas. Popularly called "Juneteenth," June 19th is celebrated as Emancipation Day in Texas with picnics, dances and political rallies.

What were people like in the community?

Everybody was very nice. We'd all get together and play ball, or run. That's about all we used to do back then. When one of us got out of hand, Miss Cunningham would send us home. "Go tell your grandmother that you did something wrong." It didn't do any good to tell Grandma that I didn't do it. She would say, "Miss Cunningham doesn't lie to me."

What kind of games did you play?

We hunted. We played baseball. Very little football. We didn't have basketball or tennis. We had a vacant lot or field that we played in and we made our own balls and bats and things. I started playing baseball with the older boys and I thought I was pretty good. If the black people were going into the major leagues in those days, I think I could have gone in. You had to have friends to compete, and in the neighborhood, well that was the whole family. We really enjoyed ourselves.

What family holidays did you celebrate?

We always celebrated the 4th of July and the black people's day, the 19th of June. People in those days would get together and we'd have like one big picnic. Every family would bring out a dinner and something to drink such as lemonade. I don't think I knew what Kool Aid was. All the farmers would get together and pitch in and buy a calf and barbecue it. There was one long table and everybody ate free.

I've done a few barbecues myself. I built a pit in the ground, put bars across and put the meat there. It would take eight to twelve hours to cook the meat, and that was real barbecue. What made it so good was because every day was work with us and we didn't have holidays that often. Thanksgiving, Christmas, the 19th of June. This was a great day with me because of plenty of food and no work that day.

What was your favorite subject in school?

History. I loved history. We had a chance to read about France and Germany. In the Army, I had a chance to visit them and Japan, Manila, Guam, Okinawa. I was in some parts of Africa.

I left home at an early age. Instead of staying in school, I wanted to get a job. I wanted to be a mortician. When I was a kid, I had one wide board and a lot of sardine cans I tied on strings behind that. Whatever died at the house, I'd put it on this board and pull it with the tin cans tied behind it and have a funeral. I had a graveyard up in the sand field and my spade stuck in the ground,

and I'd bury this thing, whatever it was, and put a cross on it.

There was an undertaker in Seguin who told me, "When you come out of school, why don't you come work for me. I can give you as much as five dollars a body when people die. I can teach you how to dress a body. You may not ever be a mortician but you can be a director." This was my ambition, to work with the dead. I came to San Antonio to ask my father for the money to go to college. I think the tuition to college for what I wanted to study was around $250 a year.

My father said, "Well, you damn fool. If you want to be a doctor or something like that, I'd put the money out for you. But I ain't gonna give you nothing to be an undertaker." He discouraged me. I had a chance to go to school and work my way through, but I lost all courage

153

John's father

after he spoke to me like that. I said, "Well, I'll go get me a job."

Times was hard. I was making $9.50 a week, working at a filling station.

Picking cotton, chopping cotton. I've done about everything to make an honest living that I could do. I wasn't a professional at anything, but I worked hard. They were building the stadium and the days they wasn't blasting rocks we went down there and worked. That was three dollars a day when we worked there.

This is why I can come to you and say, don't let anybody disappoint you about an education. The older you get, the more you will need it. I don't think anyone, white or black or anyone else, held me back. I think I held my own self back. At one time I had a teacher, Miss Maggie Phillips. Miss Phillips had one arm but she was a beautiful teacher. She could enlighten students so much by the things she'd tell us. She could sew and do beautiful seamstitching with just one hand. She mentioned so many times that she would drop something and she'd reach down to grab it, and her hand wouldn't be there. She said, "That's the same way you'll be if you don't get a full education. You're going to reach for something and you won't have that educational arm or hand to grasp it."

Did you draw when you were young?

Yes, I did. I always loved to draw. But I did not have as much interest as I do now. I really started drawing in 1981. When I was a kid we didn't have art in school like you do now. The reason why

154

I didn't take up art any sooner was on account of having jobs and working for a living.

What materials did you work with?

I used whatever I could get my hands on. Anything that I could pick up to draw on I would use. I used pencils. You can take strawberries and make a color, but we didn't have colors like you have today. We had ink that you filled your pens with, but we had pencils mostly. We had a blackboard and eraser.

Is that a picture of your grandfather?

Actually, no. But in one way yes. In a way this kind of resembles my grandfather. My grandfather was tall. You see that boy in the background? You can say that was me. An artist always has himself in any picture that he draws. He's a part of anything that he does, part of that picture. When I do these things, they're things that I remember. I think if you take up art on your own and do it from your own self experience and in your own way, it just seems to me that you can get the story of your art out better.

I'd like to take you on a field trip. We'd go down to the old part of the country that I'm acquainted with and see old buildings and old wagons and things that were left there. It's changed quite a bit now from what it was. The people aren't living there now. They've moved

away. Most of the houses are empty. Down in that old town, it's like a haunted place now. Just one store now, where I have seen life and people.

I love old things. I like to go around old vacant houses and just walk in there and look, and stand by myself. Sounds like I can hear voices of old people coming back. I look at old pans and pots laying over there and wonder what did they use them for and who cooked with these.

These visions come, but I don't tell anybody about them. I go sit under a tree and just sit there and be quiet. Just rear back against it. And the wind just

155

whispers through the leaves and the limbs. It quietly talks to you. An old live oak tree has a long story behind it. Everything upon the face of the earth has a meaning.

Do you feel that you've influenced your children and grandchildren to draw?

I don't think I have a child who has an interest in drawing. It was mostly my grandchildren. When they come out to the house, every one of them wants to draw. We all sit in the kitchen, and help ourselves from the box there where I give them pieces of drawing colors. I have papers there they pass around, and I let them draw on their own, whatever they want to make. I have two grand-daughters I think will be pretty good if they keep it in their minds. But I really want them to learn on their own. I think a person's mind in general, if you make up your mind strong enough to do something, you can. I believe you can. I believe you can do anything you want to, but fly.

Maggie Cousins

Maggie Cousins was the daughter of the first pharmacist in Munday, Texas. An early and avid reader, she sought her fortune in New York where she became a successful writer and editor, and an acquaintance of the most important literary figures of her time. She now lives in San Antonio and is still engaged in reading and writing.

Maggie with her mother and brother.

Maggie Cousins

What was Texas like when you were a child?

When I was under five, I lived in a very small town, Munday, in the western part of the state. It was surrounded by ranches, and it was dry and hot. Summer was burning hot. Winter was freezing cold. There was very little spring and no fall because there weren't any trees. I thought it was wonderful.

We had a dugout and we were often in it, especially during the spring when there were thunderstorms and tornadoes. They could come in the middle of the night when nobody expected them. I remember my father carrying me to the storm cellar. There were two-by-fours rushing past us and he was frightened. I

159

thought it was exciting—lightning and thunder.

My mother had a horror of the house falling over on the door of the dugout or storm cellar so that we couldn't get out. So we had two doors, one facing the front and one facing the back.

Once when they left me with the hired girl, there came a terrible storm. She was a good Catholic girl and got her holy water and sprinkled us both down with it. That's why we weren't struck by lightning.

Sometimes people who hadn't got storm cellars would appear at the door in the middle of incredible hail and thunder and lightning. We always had them in. We kept a five-gallon crock of fresh water in the cellar during storm season.

There were lots of tramps, hoboes, and since my mother was incapable of turning down anyone she knew was hungry, she would give them food. They followed the railroad track, and they would mark the gate if they got

good food there so that the next hobo would go there, too. My father sometimes had to work at night so there wouldn't be a man at home. Once my mother fixed this man a plate of food and put it on the broom and put it out the door. There was no welfare in those days. Some tramps were looking for work, and some were just hoboes that lived on the roads.

What were your friends like?

I didn't have any children to play with, but I had Grandpa and Grandma and aunts and people who had time to talk to me. They told me stories. That's one reason I became a writer. I didn't know anyone my own age.

I had an imaginary playmate before my brother was born. It was not a person; it was a horse. My father and mother couldn't do anything about it. They let my imaginary horse eat at the table and put out oats for it. I had that horse for years. When my brother was born it just left me. It flew off with wings. I think I must have read something about Pegasus. Once in a while I'd see him again in my sleep.

I used to run away to my grandmother's house. She lived across the pasture, and she had two teenage daughters who were still in school. They petted me and gave me ribbons out of their candy boxes their beaux brought them,

Maggie's father.

He'd say, "You walked over here, you can walk home."

Were you always interested in writing?

My father and mother read books and magazines and I saw them reading and I would sit with my books. I couldn't read, and I thought, "They must get something out of it that I don't get." I began to see letters made words, and I learned the alphabet off of things like Bon Ami soap and Calumet baking powder. I would ask what they meant. My father had a drug store and he had a lot of drug jars that had Latin names and I learned to read from them when I was about four.

My father went to market, which was Dallas, to buy holiday goods for the drugstore. He bought me this beautiful book, Robert Louis Stevenson's *A Child's Garden of Verses*. It was gorgeous. It had a dark green suede back with watered-silk end papers and beautiful illustrations. It was so fine my mother put it in the parlor. She wouldn't let me carry it around. I memorized everything in it. All

and little tongs, hair ribbons and everything. It was the only place I had to run away to. My father didn't like me to run away. He would get me and make me walk home. I'd get stickers in my feet, and it was too hot, and I'd start begging.

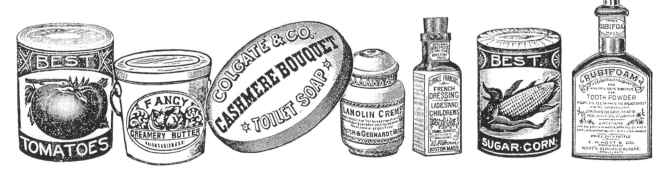

Munday, Texas

In 1905 Munday had a population of about 400 and no positive assurance of a railroad. All merchandise was freighted from Stamford or Seymour, 42 or 33 miles away respectively. There were three general merchandise stores, two small drugstores, a few smaller mercantile establishments, a small bank building, one gin, and three blacksmith shops. From the time the first train glided into town June 6, 1906, new business sprang up. The splendid passenger train of the railroad made a daily round trip from Abilene to Wichita Falls. Munday, by 1907, had become a town of 1500 to 2000 inhabitants. All of this change had come about in the twenty months after the railroad arrived.

—from *The History of Wichita Falls*

my life I wanted to go to London because of that book. When I got there I expected it to be exactly like Stevenson said. I kept waiting for the lamplighters to come.

I read everything. We didn't have many books because they were expensive and there weren't that many published, but they wrote good books for children. I was reading one of them the other day. *Rebecca of Sunnybrook Farm.* My favorite maxim came from that book. "When joy and beauty clash, let beauty go smash."

I always got books for Christmas because I asked for them. And dolls. My father bought dolls and toys from the drugstore, European dolls when he could get them. I had a life-sized baby doll with real hair and eyelashes, and it cried, and you could feed it.

But I always wanted books and I usually knew which ones I wanted. I had an aunt who also gave me good books, *Wind in the Willows* and Kipling's *Jungle Book.*

The Wizard of Oz by Frank Baum

She was married and had four small children but she knew the kind of books that I liked.

I didn't go to school until we moved to Wichita Falls, and I went to the second grade because I was able to read. I was delighted to be among people my own age. My teacher was Miss Jennie and she read to us after lunch. She read us all the Oz books. That was the best part of the day for all of us.

Since I always enjoyed books, I wanted to have something to do with them. I didn't know what being a writer meant, but I used to think, I want books that are about people like us so that I could identify with them. I never remember any time in my life that I didn't want to do something about reading and writing. I enjoyed it so much. It's something that carries you away, like the Oz books. I believed it was real, the Emerald City and the Wicked Witch of the West. I believed in that.

How did you help out at home?

My mother had a card club, and I was allowed to put on my best dress and walk around with the punch and when they changed tables, I was supposed to punch these tallies. I liked the refreshments so I didn't complain too much.

We had a big farm house not very far from town, but it was a full-time job to run that kind of house. About five o'clock in the morning my father milked the cows. Breakfast was ham and eggs and grits and hot biscuits. Then everything was cleaned up and the house was scoured down, and then they cooked dinner.

There wasn't any bread to buy when I was a little girl. You had to make your own bread. The days of the week were divided. Monday, laundry. Tuesday, ironing. Wednesday, polishing silver and all that. Thursday was Mother's day to go calling. It was a little town, and they all had calling cards. Friday was baking day. They made bread and rolls, buns and coffee cakes. My mother usually made the cakes and pies because she was good at that. Women prided themselves on being able to cook. If you couldn't cook, you couldn't talk to other women.

Saturday they got ready for Sunday, because church was all day. You went to church and came home to dinner, and you went back to church at night. Sometimes you could go driving in the buggy, or go to see the train come through. The train came through at six

DIPHTHERIA

KEEP OUT OF THIS HOUSE

By Order of BOARD OF HEALTH

_____

HEALTH OFFICER

o'clock and everybody got dressed up, had their horses drawn up, the buggies in a row, to see the train come through.

Many domestic tasks have disappeared forever, like dishwashing, laundry, hanging out the clothes, ironing, beating the rugs, beating the mattresses, and spring cleaning. I think women were happy in those days because they had a role that was demanding and valuable and important to the people who lived in the house. I certainly don't recommend it now, but there was a quality to it, and the rhythm might have been part of it. I'm not sure there's any spring ritual any more.

What happened when you got sick?

They didn't know anything about communicable diseases and they had epidemics. The scourge of the country was smallpox. If smallpox broke out, they put a sign on the gate, and everybody would walk a block out of the way to keep from going past the house.

Smallpox was very serious. Many people died and the rest were often disfigured by it. They had a pesthouse in Munday. People who got smallpox were sent to the pesthouse where they had to just lie around.

My father was vaccinated in the public square because there was a great fear of putting into your own blood the blood of some disease. So my father was vaccinated and it swayed people to let their children be vaccinated. They dug a large hole in his arm and poured the vaccine in it. His arm swelled up and he was terribly sick, but he didn't ever have smallpox.

One of my uncles, who was a cow-puncher at the time, got smallpox and they sent him to the pesthouse. My father was able to see him and take food to him because of his vaccination. He and the doctor were the only people who went there. My uncle told my father he didn't want his face pitted because he was very handsome. "Tie my hands at night so I won't scratch myself." They

164

tied him up every night but he got loose one night and he scratched a tiny pit on the end of his nose. I used to ask about it and he said, "I'm going to have a diamond put in it."

Almost every child had whooping cough, measles, scarlet fever, diphtheria. I had all of those. I was the first child in Knox County to have scarlet fever. They thought I contracted it in Seymour, Texas, where I'd been taken for a fancy haircut. They brushed the back of my hair, and the doctor said he believed I got it from the brush.

They thought I was going to die for two or three days, but then I pulled through. There was a long convalescence with all my aunts bringing dolls and Japanese fans and pots of roses, delicious food, custard and all that. It was very exciting.

Then we had to get out of our house. We went to Wichita Falls and spent a week while they burned raw sulfur in the rooms. It was the only way they had to kill germs. Everything in the house had to be washed and cleaned or thrown away. Everything.

My father was a pharmacist and knew every doctor in West Texas. I had the best medical attention and all there was to have. There just wasn't any. People were operated on the kitchen table in those days. I knew doctors who cut open a patient in the kitchen. They gave them chloroform.

What kind of games did you play?

After we moved to Dallas, I was in the fourth grade, we played every night around the lamppost. That's the way we met boys. When you got ready to go with a boy, you went with somebody you'd known all your life. When your mother called you, usually at nine o'clock, you had to go. Some mothers had a whistle.

When I was ten or twelve we used to ride the fire wagon. We jumped on the back of it. I was taken to the police station in Highland Park because we were riding the fire truck. They were very severe with us because we could have been killed They called our families to come get us. That was the worst part, their coming.

We used to go bug-hunting in the summer, in Mr. Nicholson's garden. He was the biggest florist in town. He had a bank of red tulips, and the boys cut those tulips and gave them to me because I was the only girl. It was thrilling. I got home and my mother said, "Where did those come from?" I said, "We went bug-hunting in Mr. Nicholson's garden." She put the tulips in vases, and the house was filled with them. Every time anybody came, delivery boys, laundress, friends, they would say, "Where did you get those?" My mother would say, "Margaret stole them." I have never stolen any other flowers. I quit stealing then.

My parents expected me to be honest, decent, truthful, and my father expected me to work. He always thought in terms of a working career for me. That was very unusual. He insisted on my being able to earn a living. I had to learn to type when I was in high school.

I wanted to be the editor of a women's magazine because they meant so much to my mother out on the prairie. When the *Ladies Home Journal* came, that was a big day. It was a lifeline to the world and the kind of culture that was denied her in that western place. There were very few women editors. They're still almost all men. I was managing editor of *Good Housekeeping* and *McCall's*. I was trained to be an editor and I expected to be one. But when the job as editor opened up, the chairman of the board said, "I'll never give the job to a woman." I resigned that day. It has changed now. It would be against the law to say that to me now.

What did your parents expect of you?

My father and mother expected life to be glorious. We didn't know people who were depressed or committed suicide. Everybody we knew worked hard. They went to church on Sunday, had picnics in the fall and celebrations on Halloween. They didn't know anybody who didn't have expectations and they expected to have to fulfill them for themselves. They didn't think much about money or power. It was character they thought about. A banker's character was more important than his money.

The worst thing that could be said about anybody was that they were useless. That was the absolute—that was a damning statement. I always wanted to be useful. I still want to be useful. I had a good time. I intended to have a good time. If you want to have an exciting life, you have to plan to have it exciting. You have to be available. You have to learn how to keep your ears and eyes open and pursue adventure.

Maggie as a young career woman, 1926

I think if you don't plan to have magic in your life, you won't have it. When I came to San Antonio, I decided to have an adventure every day. If I lived in Munday, I'd manage to have an adventure every day, if I made up my mind. I'll never get bored until I haven't got time to have an adventure.

Ideas
and
Activities

Thinking Historically...

Use these ideas to begin your own oral history collections. Copy these pages or use the ones in this book to get you started. Add ideas of your own. Start a project in your family, your class or your neighborhood. Watch your collection grow.

Begin with an idea that you are especially interested in or curious about~favorite foods, money, first jobs, transportation, rules about going to bed, family mealtimes, embarrassing moments~then interview lots of people about what that one thing was like when they were your age.

Use this space to make notes.

Compare all your answers. What new ideas do they give you? Do you want to try some of them out for yourself?

2 **Where did your family come from? Make an audio tape collection about the history of your family coming to America. Find out how many generations of your family have been in the United States. What country, or countries, did your family come from? Did your parents or grandparents grow up some place that was very different? What was it like? How was it different?**

Start by making a list of interview questions. You might think of more questions than you will use. Use the space below to write them:

. . . .

. . . .

. . . .

. . . .

. . . .

. . . .

. . . .

IMPORTANT NOTE: Listen very closely to the person you are interviewing. You will get ideas for more questions from what the person is saying. Begin your tape by stating the name of the person you are interviewing and the date. That information will help you later when you are organizing your collection.

3 **Make a class collection. Add together the information from each member of your class. How many countries are represented?**
~Compare holidays, games, food . . . what else?
~Make a map that shows the route that each family took to get to the United States or the particular state you live in.
~Make a big chart that compares all the differences you found.

Make a family collection. Make some copies of this page and the next and use them to interview several older people in your family. Then cut and fold them together to make a small book about each person.

pets

When I Was Just Your Age

an interview with

_____

by

_____

8

(CUT)

school

holidays

4

5

(FOLD HERE)

(CUT HERE)

173

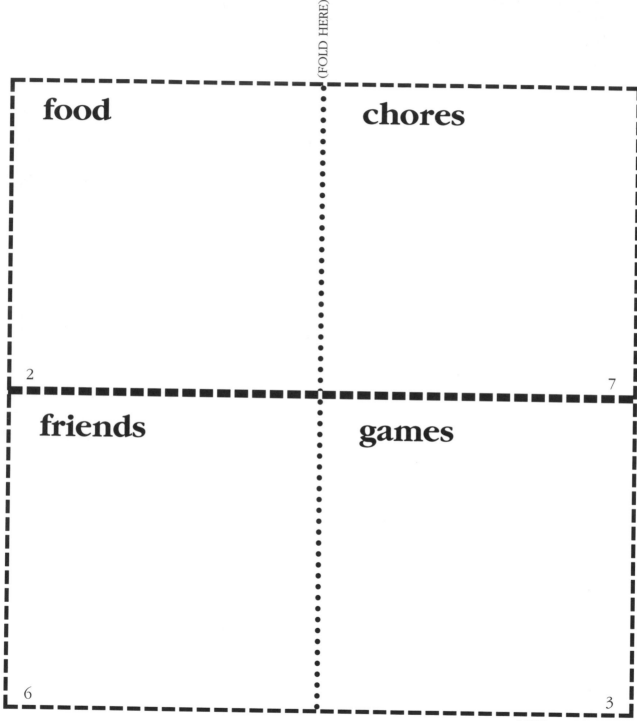

(FOLD HERE)

food

chores

2

7

friends

games

6

3

(CUT HERE)

 Begin to write your own story. Keep a journal. You will enjoy reading back over it as you go along. It will give you ideas . . . and someday, you might want to share it with your own children.

Here are some ideas to get you started:

First Journal Notes of _____

on this date of _____

What does it mean to be a member of the _____ family?

What does it mean to be a citizen of your state at this time in history? How do you think it is different from other places?

What are your pressures, worries, hopes?

What is important for you to do? To have? To be?